I0450755

DEATH WALKS A DOG

A PENELOPE STANDING MYSTERY

TESS BAYTREE

SPECULATIVE TURTLE PRESS

*P*enelope Standing tugged her ski cap down over her silvering hair, hoping that her target would get a little closer before discovering her. Mayor Harrison wasn't known for taking the long route between his office and the nearby cafe, but he'd make a change if he saw her too soon.

Flanking the mayor on his left was the acting chief of police, Jake Wheeler. He had a folder in one hand, probably the budget he'd been trying to get Harrison to sign off on for the last two weeks. In general, Penelope considered it unfair that men were considered more distinguished when they added laugh lines and grey hair, but she was willing to make an exception in this particular case. She knew the exact point Jake saw her from the slight hitch in his stride, but aside from raising one eyebrow he didn't do anything. The giddiness she felt at the sight of him after over two years together still caught her by surprise.

A smattering of other people enjoying the spring sunshine helped her blend in, and she saw the mayor take his usual path between the concrete planters. Now he was trapped.

Jumping to her feet, Penelope took a deep breath, pitched her voice to carry to the edges of the tiny park, and channeled her inner Janis Joplin.

"Oh Lord, won't you give me, the confidence of this man," she sang, rushing the syllables to make it fit the tune. Two men in suits sitting nearby glanced at her, then away, an immediate dismissal she was getting used to now that she'd hit fifty. A teenager on the other side of the path pulled out his phone and started recording.

She took another breath and continued. "He's so mediocre, I can't understand. He stole people's houses, and got elected again." She didn't *quite* hit the high note, but she thought the spirit of Janis would forgive her. "Oh Lord, won't you give me / the confidence of this man." It really *didn't* scan correctly, she decided.

As she finished the first verse, Penelope looked to her right to see that Mayor Harrison had stopped walking and was staring at her, lips pursed. Penelope took another breath. "Oh Lord, can you end this man's explaining to me. He dropped out of high school. I have a degree. Worked too hard all my life, to heed idiocy. Oh Lord —"

A bellow cut her off. "That's it!" The mayor's face was flushed. "This is harassment. Every day it's something else. That stupid ad in the paper lost me investors. I'm *still* finding glitter in the goddamn bathtub!" He turned to the man next to him. "Arrest her!"

Jake paused and rocked back on his heels. "Your Honor." He scratched one brow. "I'm not sure that bad rhyming and out-of-key singing are crimes, technically."

Penelope straightened. "Bad rhyming? I'd like to see you do better, Mr. 'Roses are red, violets are blue, I can't finish this because I have to go to a training class on resuscitating people'."

"That's not exactly —," Jake started, before the mayor cut him off.

"I don't care what you have to do, just make her shut up!"

Jake cleared his throat. "Sir, there's only one thing I can think of that will make Ms. Standing stop talking, and then I'd have to arrest her for doing it here in public." His voice trailed off as the mayor stomped down the path toward the cafe.

Penelope stared at Jake.

He smiled. "There's an ordinance against sleeping in this park. What did you think I was talking about?"

Penelope shook her head. "Nice try, Slick." Her phone beeped. "I have to go see a dog about a walk. We still on for dinner tonight?"

"If I'm not there right away, there's still a bottle of wine chilling in the refrigerator."

Penelope blew him a kiss as she waltzed away.

TWO STREETS down and one to the side, the mayor's recently divorced wife, Jezza Harrison, lived alone in a tiny nineteenth century cottage. It had originally been built for the mother-in-law of the town's founder, and now was one of the few Victorians remaining. Unlike the larger houses from the same period, this house was painted in a cheery yellow and red polychrome. Penelope had once counted six different colors of paint delineating the various features, and was relieved she wasn't the one responsible for maintaining that splendor. Despite the size of the cottage, Jezza seemed happy to be living in a house that her husband hadn't had a hand in. "I'll be damned if I keep living in one of those monstrosities he builds," she had told Penelope three months earlier when she'd hired her to walk the dog. "But there's not enough room for Brutus in this house unless he gets more exercise, and it'll really chafe the troll's hide when he finds out his money is paying your wages."

Brutus, the world's most ill-behaved mastiff, had become The Thing that both halves of the couple wanted, or at least wanted the other half not to possess. Penelope couldn't understand why one person, much less two, would want a dog that weighed as much as a full grown man, left ropes of drool in his wake, and couldn't be reliably house-trained. Nevertheless, it had taken a judge's threats to force the couple to come up with a custody arrangement they could both live with.

As she walked briskly up the driveway, Penelope checked the time. Five minutes later than planned. If Jezza had been home, that might have been a problem, but Penelope had heard Brutus barking from a block away. That meant his owner wasn't there. As Penelope put the key in the lock, Brutus's barks of loneliness turned to growls of protection. It would have been a scary sound if she hadn't seen him run backwards into a chair when a new handyman had come by. "Relax, buddy, it's just me," she called through the door. Brutus's deep growls turned to quieter whines.

The smell of dog poop hit her like a wave when she cracked opened the door, so it wasn't a surprise to see paw prints all over the normally immaculate hardwood floor. Taking a deep breath of fresh air, Penelope pushed her way into the entrance hall, slammed the door behind her, and tiptoed across the living room, one hand on Brutus's head to keep him from jumping on her. From the looks of things, he'd had an accident soon after Jezza had left him in the morning, and then spent the intervening time tracking it all over the house.

Fifteen minutes later Brutus had clean feet, and the worst of the mess on the floor had been cleaned up with paper towels and a spray bottle of citrus-based cleaner. Technically it wasn't Penelope's job to clean up the house — she'd been hired to walk Brutus, not house-sit — but Jezza was a steady client who paid her bills, and that meant keeping her happy. If Penelope did a fast mop of the worst areas, the floor would be dry again by the time she and Brutus came back from their walk and she'd only be a few minutes late for her next appointment.

"Where does your mom keep the mop, buddy?" she asked the dog who was now sprawled on the couch with a stuffed shark under his chin. Penelope opened the closet next to the front door, and found only coats.

Jezza was usually home when Penelope came to walk Brutus, so this was the first time Penelope had really gotten a chance to look through the house. She'd seen walk-in closets bigger than the Victorian-era bedrooms, but there was a certain charm to the multi-paned windows and crown molding accenting the rooms. At some point in the past, probably before the house had been listed with the historical society, the bathroom had been remodeled to include a shower. The wall of the house had been bumped out for extra space, and the room divided to make a laundry room. That was where Penelope tracked the scent of bleach and finally found the supplies she'd been searching for.

She froze with her hand on the mop, all thoughts of cleaning up gone.

Jezza's lifeless body lay sprawled in the laundry room sink.

CHAPTER 2

*S*itting on a stone bench in Jezza's garden, Brutus leashed by her side, Penelope decided that an extended sit-stay was just as boring as the dogs made it out to be. Her 911 call had led to one patrol car, which had led to more cars, and then the coroner and a crime scene van. Throughout it all she had waited patiently where the first officer had asked her to sit, but she had started to believe they'd forgotten all about her. She was trying to decide if texting Jake to speed up the process would be taking advantage of the relationship or not, when she saw Brian walk up to the house. She and Jake had gone out to dinner with the lieutenant and his wife just the week before.

"Brian!" Penelope dashed forward, then had to stop and haul back on the leash to keep Brutus from barreling through a knot of people. "Hey, is there any way I can get out of here? I need to go give a cat some insulin."

"You're the one who found her?" Brian took a step back from the dog. "Let me grab someone to take a quick state-ment." He waved his arm. "Dolan! I have a job for you." He waited until a young man in uniform hustled forward. "Get an initial statement from Ms. Standing so she can leave." He put an arm out to stop the man from heading into the house. "Outside. Talk to her outside. Assume the entire house is a crime scene." Someone called his name and he turned, dismissing them both.

Penelope spelled her name and gave her phone number, but as she explained how she had found the body, Officer Dolan frowned.

"And how did you know the mayor's wife?"

"Jezza hired me to walk her dog." Penelope dug out a business card from her pocket and gave it to him. In plain script it read *Penelope Standing Services: Pet Sitting, Dog Walking, and More!* That last part included picking up dry cleaning, baking hypoallergenic dog treats for an elderly poodle, and even helping deliver the mail. The phrasing had occasionally led to some unwarranted conclusions, but only once had she needed to explain, in person, that the *and More!* didn't include anything that required either party to remove clothing. "That's what I do for a living."

"The mayor's wife, was she good to work for? Did you have any problems with her?"

"Jezza."

He looked up from his notebook. "Yes?"

"Her name was Jezza. She didn't get her identity from some man, you know." Warming to her subject, Penelope waved her arm to indicate the house. "She had... dreams. And... ambitions. And..." Penelope waved her arm again as she realized she actually knew almost nothing about the woman. "And she hated huge houses!" she added triumphantly.

The young man hitched up his weapons belt and leaned toward her. "Wonderful. Now can you tell me where you were today?"

"What time?"

7

After a brief pause, he answered. "All day. Since you got up."

"Fine. I got up about six-thirty."

"And were you alone?"

"No, I was with my boyfriend."

He flipped a page. "And this boyfriend's name?"

Penelope raised her chin. "Jake." She recited his phone number but deliberately didn't give Jake's last name. "And then I got to the Episcopalian church by seven." Penelope went through her schedule on her phone, ending with when she had shown up to walk Brutus.

There was a moment of silence as Officer Dolan finished writing. "So other than during church, nobody can verify where you were this morning."

"Not during church, either, if it comes to that. I take care of the reverend's Dalmatian while he's busy, so I wasn't actually in the church." She saw Brian walk by inside the house. "Brian, can I go now? Who's going to be in charge of the dog until the mayor picks him up?"

Brian waved her away. "Talk to you later, Pen. Dolan, you're in charge of the dog. Don't let it inside the house."

Penelope shoved the leash into the officer's hand. "He's a nice dog."

"Wait." He took a few steps toward the house. "Sir, can I talk to you first?"

Brutus made a break for the open door and dragged the unprepared Dolan behind him. As Penelope hurried away she was treated to the sounds of multiple people yelling about getting the dog out of their crime scene.

* * *

AFTER HAROLD the cat had finished scolding her for being late with his mid-day meal, insulin, and chin-scratching,

Penelope went across the alley to pick up Heidi for her daily three mile run. She had just clipped on the leash when her phone vibrated and Rod Stewart sang "If you want my body and you think I'm sexy…"

"Hi Jake."

"I leave you alone for less than an hour and I have my newest patrolman calling to confirm that I was with you in bed this morning."

Penelope smiled as she locked the door and walked briskly along the sidewalk to warm up. "I hope you drew him a picture. At what point did he realize who he was talking to?"

"Well, he suddenly got real quiet when I was spelling my last name for him. I'm assuming that if you were feeling irritated enough to do that to him that you're okay…"

Penelope picked up the pace to a slow jog, Heidi matching her speed. "I'm fine. It mostly just surprised me. She wasn't a close friend or anything." She grimaced. "I sort of accidentally cleaned up the crime scene before I found her, though."

"Of course you did."

Penelope's phone beeped. "I've got to go. I'll tell you about it over dinner. Love you." She switched calls and sped up. "This is Penelope."

"Mom, are you running from the cops or something?" Her son was just barely audible over a background of other excited voices.

"Nope, just running. How's testing the new game going?" Her son's company was trying to cash in on one of the periodic retro crazes with an updated version of *Oregon Trail*, using landmarks from a famous series of movies, without actually using the names in order to avoid licensing fees.

"I just got killed in a trash compactor, so I'm taking a quick break. I guess this means that you didn't really kill the mayor's wife then."

9

Penelope frowned and hopped over a large crack in the pavement. Heidi extended her stride to match her. "Seth, you know women aren't defined by the men in their lives, right?"

Her son laughed. "Chill, Mom. I know. I just never met her so I don't know her name. Jimmy called to tell me that he saw you talking to the police and that the mayor's wife had been murdered. Forgive me. I promise I'll send a donation to Planned Parenthood to make things right." A shout and a chorus of wails came through the phone. "Mostly I was calling to make sure it wasn't the mayor who died and that you didn't need a lawyer."

Penelope lengthened her stride to avoid the worst of a sidewalk buckled by tree roots. "I think I should be okay, but I appreciate the thought."

"Okay, just checking." Another yell pierced the background. "Oops, Richard just got digested by a moon worm. I need to get back to work. Talk to you soon."

Penelope removed her earpiece as she ran. She looked down at the dog loping along next to her. "My son gets paid good money to play video games." Heidi flicked her ears to the side. "What an odd world it is."

CHAPTER 3

*S*nuggled up against Jake on his couch after dinner, Penelope thought back to her conversation with Officer Dolan. "Did you ever meet Jezza?"

He kept his eyes on the television. "I talked to her a few times." On the screen a smattering of muted applause followed a swing, and the camera followed the arc of the ball as it landed on the green.

"But you didn't know her well?"

"Not really. I saw her a handful of times before she and her husband separated, mostly when she visited him at his office." Jake paused the replay and looked at her. "Why?"

She shrugged. "I got all irritated with that man-child taking my statement today because he kept calling her 'the mayor's wife', like she didn't have any identity of her own, but I realized I've been doing the same thing for the last three months. I don't know anything about her. I'm such a hypocrite."

"It's probably just as well you two weren't close," Jake said, clicking the remote again. "This way you just look clueless instead of malicious."

"Excuse me?" Penelope struggled to sit up straighter.

One side of Jake's mouth twitched, but he kept his eyes on the screen. "Well, there wasn't a forced entry and you have the key, the dog knows you, and you couldn't have contaminated the scene more thoroughly if you'd tried." He pulled her closer and kissed the top of her head. "But the good news is that the coroner put time of death between four-thirty and six-thirty and you have a really strong alibi."

Penelope settled back again. "Mmm, thank god I planned ahead and seduced you two years ago."

Jake picked up the nearly empty wine bottle at his foot and emptied it into her glass. "Is that what happened? I always thought it was the other way around."

"Ha! With your moves? Not a chance." Penelope lifted her head and took a sip of wine. "Isn't it always the spouse anyway? I bet he did it."

"Nope. Turns out our mayor suffers from insomnia —"

"Because he has a guilty conscience."

Jake continued as if she hadn't interrupted. "— and he was having a sleep study done last night. Two people watched him sleep. And they have a recording."

Penelope sighed. "I guess that would be pretty hard to fake." She tried to keep the disappointment from her voice.

Jake leaned over to set the remote on the coffee table. "Besides, I think he still felt something for her. He was pretty upset when he found out she was dead."

Penelope groaned and slid down on the couch, keeping her wine glass level. "I'm going to have to be nice to him for a while, aren't I?"

"If it makes you feel any better, he tried to pin it on you, too."

"Bastard." She closed her eyes. "Wake me up when they get to the interesting part."

CHAPTER 4

*W*hen Penelope knocked on the back door to the rectory the next morning, she was greeted by a yelp and clatter of something that sounded like shoes falling onto the floor. Taking that as an invitation to enter, she opened the door carefully and stepped in. Normally unflappable, Reverend CJ Miller had the look of a man who had jumped out of bed just moments before. His weathered face, usually smooth-shaven at this time of the day and sporting bits of tissue to stanch the bleeding from various nicks, showed a grey stubble.

"Come in, come in," he said, as he hopped across the room on one shod foot to sit down at the kitchen table where the other sock waited. His elderly Dalmatian lay on the floor next to the oven, nose pressed up against her empty food bowl. "Do you mind feeding Spot this morning? I'm running behind."

"No problem." Penelope opened the pantry, found the dog food among the neatly stacked dry goods, and started dishing out the kibble. Spot didn't get up, but her tail slapped against the linoleum. "Late night?"

"No, I just overslept." He nodded toward the dog. "Nature's alarm clock failed me. At this rate I'm going to have to start setting my oven timer to wake me up again."

Penelope laughed. "You've been trusting your dog to get you up on time?" She put Spot's bowl down in front of her and scratched the Dalmatian's left ear before standing up and leaving her to her breakfast.

"No, I've been trusting Jezza to get me up on time. May she rest in peace," the reverend added in an automatic addition. He glanced up and smiled at Penelope's look. "Sounds bad when I put it that way, doesn't it? But ever since Jezza moved in, she's been letting Brutus out at five-thirty on the dot every morning. Or at least every weekday. You can just see the corner of that yard from the second floor. Spot barks at Brutus from my bedroom window. Brutus wasn't there this morning, so Spot didn't wake me up. Someone is taking care of Brutus… Oh yes, of course, the mayor must have him," he said, answering his own question. He finished tying his shoe, stood up, and took a large gulp of coffee. "Right, I think I'm ready." Keys jingled as he patted his pocket, and he tapped the glasses hanging from a chain around his neck. Spot climbed to her feet and walked over to stand next to the closed door. "I'll see you in a bit."

"Preach it, padre," Penelope said with a wave. "Oh wait a second. Did Brutus and Spot wake you up yesterday?"

"Five-thirty on the dot, just like always." CJ took another gulp of coffee, maneuvered around his dog, and hurried out the door. Spot glanced back to ensure that Penelope was still there, then settled down against the door where she could sleep the sleep of ancient dogs, but still be assured nobody could get in or out of the house without waking her. Penelope poured herself a mug of coffee and sat down to think.

* * *

AFTER THE SERVICE, Penelope waited in the kitchen, sitting on the floor with Spot draped over her lap until Mrs. Tillman's Cadillac had driven away. It wasn't that she was *avoiding* the woman, really. It was just that Mrs. Tillman, eighty if she was a day, knew Penelope didn't have a car, and got offended if Penelope turned down her offer to drive her wherever she was going. Mrs. Tillman only lived two blocks away, and everyone on the route knew to watch out for her as she inched her way down the street at fifteen miles per hour under the speed limit. Having her drive an unfamiliar route to drop Penelope off would have been tempting fate. Besides, it was faster to walk.

CJ bent to look out the window. "Coast is clear."

Penelope extracted herself from under the Dalmatian. "Thanks. See you tomorrow!" She jogged down the steps and headed across the now-empty parking lot. An unmarked police car pulled in from the street, in a feat of timing that could only mean that the driver had either been waiting for Mrs. Tillman to leave, or Penelope to arrive. Penelope would have known it was driven by a law enforcement officer just by the way it took the corner, even if she hadn't recognized the lieutenant. Brian pulled up next to her. "Morning, Pen. Do you have a few minutes?" He leaned over and opened the passenger door.

Penelope nodded, then stopped halfway in. "Wait, this isn't about me not telling Officer Dolan who Jake was, is it?"

Brian laughed. "Are you kidding? Half the squad wants to buy you a beer. I did have to promise Dolan that he could be the one to cuff you if it turns out you did it, though."

"Seems only fair." Penelope buckled her seat belt and closed the door, then hung onto the door handle as Brian accelerated out of the parking lot and made a quick turn onto the next street, stopping in front of Jezza's house.

They got out of the car. "Do you mind doing a quick

walk-through with me to show me exactly what you did yesterday and let me know if anything is out of place?" Brian lifted up the yellow tape in front of the walkway to allow her to duck under. "You came in through the front door? Was the door locked?"

Penelope pulled out her key ring and picked out the one with "Br" scribbled on blue tape. "I don't think I even checked. I could hear Brutus barking, and he only did that when Jezza wasn't there. I just assumed it *would* be locked." Brian motioned her on so she inserted the key in the door, turned, and pushed. The door stayed closed. "The deadbolt wasn't on yesterday."

"Did she usually lock the deadbolt?"

"No. I don't think she was that worried about security because Brutus was there." Penelope wiggled the key from the doorknob and looked up at Brian. "Not that he would ever bite anyone, but his bark is pretty scary if you don't know him."

Brian nodded. "Okay, so what did you do next?"

Penelope unlocked the deadbolt and showed him the path she'd taken to let Brutus into the yard, and explained everything she'd done. The house had black smudges around all the doors, and the floor that she'd been planning to mop the day before remained uncleaned, though the house smelled better now that it had dried out.

Brian made a few notes as she talked. "So you grabbed the leash when you went outside to wash the dog off?"

Penelope nodded. "I didn't think he would hold still otherwise."

"And the leash was…?"

Penelope pointed to the coatrack by the front door. "Right there."

"And that's where it usually was?"

She nodded before understanding why he was asking. "Is that how she was killed?"

Brian continued writing notes as he spoke. "Hit over the head and then strangled with the leash."

Penelope looked at the coatrack. "Oh."

"We found a packed overnight bag in the closet, but the clothes aren't her size. Did she ever have anyone else staying here?"

"Not that I ever knew anything about."

"Did she ever talk to you about her hobbies, who her friends were, or where she was from?"

Penelope shook her head. "We really only talked a couple of times, and that was about Brutus." Jezza had been especially proud of her dog's pedigree. He'd been sired by a mastiff with multiple championships, and one of his littermates had titled in search and rescue. Brutus, himself, had never done more than sleep on the couch and destroy things, but that hadn't seemed to bother his owner. Penelope knew far more about Brutus's family than she ever had about Jezza's. "Wouldn't her husband know all that stuff?"

Brian sighed. "Jezebel Taylor, the *real* Jezebel Taylor, died five years ago in a car crash. Nobody knows who this woman really is. Her husband claims she never talked about her past and never introduced him to anyone she'd known before she met him."

Penelope made a face. "How much would it suck to ditch one life and then end up married to Mayor Harrison? Poor woman." She shook her head. "Hang on, though, she gave me a second number in case of emergencies." Penelope went through her phone contact list. "Here it is." She read off the number to him and he repeated it back. "Oh, and the rev said that Jezza let Brutus outside yesterday morning at 5:30, just like she always did, if that helps."

Brian looked up from his notes. "Gunning for my job now, Pen?"

"And have Jake be my boss? Hardly." She glanced at the clock. "Anything else? I have a pretty full schedule."

"Call me if you think of anything."

Penelope gave a quick salute and headed off to her next client.

CHAPTER 5

ollowing the client's very long and very specific instructions, Penelope walked Ginger to the deserted dog park. "Eleven o'clock, on the dot," she told the Corgi as she took a time-stamped photo of the dog in the park and texted it to the owner. "And now I get to throw your tennis ball a minimum of fifteen times. Are you ready?" She tossed the ball in a high arc that took it nearly to the fence.

The park wasn't quite empty, she realized, as a second dog raced for the ball, but she recognized Brian and Anne's Australian Shepherd and looked around, finally locating Anne on a bench in the far corner. Penelope and Jake were friends with them as a couple, but Brian was the real connection. Most of that was because Jake and Brian worked together. But Anne occasionally implied Penelope's work walking dogs and doing necessary tasks wasn't a real job, and that she should find more traditional employment. Even so, Penelope and Anne had always been superficially friendly.

Penelope waved and walked over, one eye on the grass to avoid stepping in a mess, but most of her attention on the dogs running back to her. Both dogs were normally well-behaved, but sometimes being at the dog park was exciting enough to make any dog forget they weren't supposed to jump on people. Ginger raced back, her stumpy legs a blur, and dropped the ball on the ground. Penelope threw the ball again and then sat down on the bench.

"Your husband gave me the third degree this morning," she joked as she looked toward Anne, "but I think he finally decided I probably wouldn't have incriminated myself quite so thoroughly if I were guilty."

The corners of Anne's mouth went up, but the smile didn't reach her eyes.

Penelope stood up to throw the ball again, her brain still processing what she'd seen. Normally Anne wore almost no makeup, but this morning she was wearing a heavy coat of concealer around one eye. Penelope sat back down again. Brian had never seemed to her like someone who would hit his wife, but she'd learned a long time ago that people did surprising things. She tried to keep her voice casual. "Do you need somewhere safe to stay?"

Anne stopped watching the dogs and gestured to her face. "This? Brian didn't do this. I tripped over the dog and hit the door frame."

"If you say so." Penelope couldn't do anything more if Anne wasn't ready to get help, but she fully intended to talk to Jake about it. He was Brian's friend, but he was also Brian's boss, and he would know what to do. More than that, he would *do* it. Jake was a firm believer in protecting the community, even if that meant taking on the police union.

"No, really, Brian had nothing to do with this." Anne's voice took on a pleading note as she turned on the bench to face Penelope. "Brian doesn't know anything about this and he can't find out."

Penelope could only think of one reason Anne would be

sporting a bruise that she didn't want her husband to know about. "What you do in your personal life is your business, but if you're cheating on Brian with someone who hits you, you're making mistakes on a whole new level."

"Pen, it's not like that." Anne stopped and sighed. "Well, it's sort of like that, but he's not the one who hit me. I stopped by his house the other morning for… well, you can imagine why I was there. But these two guys broke in. They had ski masks and kept yelling at me to tell them where the money was." She shivered. "I threw my purse at them and told them to take everything. I mean, I had maybe fifteen dollars in my wallet. I thought I was dead for sure. But then they ended up leaving without taking anything at all."

"They just left?"

"Yeah, one minute they're screaming that I need to tell them where the money is, and the next thing I know, one of them says 'It's not her.' and runs out the door." Anne reached over and grabbed Penelope's wrist. "You see why we couldn't go to the police, don't you? Even if I asked them to keep it quiet, there's no way Brian wouldn't find out." Anne let go and turned to look at the dogs. "'It's not her,'" she repeated softly. "I'm an idiot. I wonder how many other women he has on the side. I thought when his wife left that we would finally be together, but it's been one excuse after another."

They sat in silence for a moment.

"How'd you hide that bruise from Brian? He's going to see it at some point, you know."

Anne shrugged. "We don't see each other that much during the week with his schedule, and I've been going to bed before he gets home. That's part of the problem. He's always working."

Penelope grimaced. "It's Mayor Harrison, isn't it?"

Anne's silence confirmed her guess.

"Anne, this could be related to Jezza. Brian needs to know."

"You can't tell him." Anne stood up and picked up her dog's leash. "He would never forgive me."

Penelope threw the ball and both dogs ran after it. "You need to find some way to tell him. Make up some story about going over there to pick up papers or something, but this could be the thing they need to catch whoever killed Jezza."

"Just stay out of it, Pen." Anne walked toward the gate and Penelope followed. "I'll deny that I ever said anything. Everyone knows you're obsessed with the man. They won't believe you."

The dogs ran up again and Penelope waited until Anne had leashed her dog and gone out of the dog park before she threw the tennis ball for the Corgi again. Behind her she heard Anne get into her car and drive away.

CHAPTER 6

"*H*ey, sexy, can I buy you a drink?"

Penelope smiled but didn't turn from her perusal of the pre-made sandwiches available at the deli counter. "Sure, but we'll have to hurry. My boyfriend will be here any minute now." She turned and looked up. "Oh, it's you." Her breath caught as Jake raised her hand to his lips without breaking eye contact. "I thought you had a budget meeting at lunch today."

He kept her hand as he reached past her to put his own lunch on the counter. "What do you want to eat? I'm buying."

Penelope regarded him out of the corner of her eye. "It's not my birthday, we've already passed Valentine's day, and as far as I know, today isn't any sort of anniversary. Yet you invited me out to lunch and you're buying." She placed a sandwich next to his and waited for him to pay. "Should I be suspicious?" The hint of embarrassment on his face had her laughing. "What did you do?"

Penelope waited until they settled at a table where Jake had a clear view of the doors. "Out with it."

"First, I promise that this is only temporary." He

unwrapped his lunch. "We're going to have a houseguest for a couple of weeks."

"Is that all?" Penelope let out the breath she was holding. "Jake, it's your house. And I have a few overnight pet sitting jobs coming up anyhow." She tried to imagine who Jake would be worried about inviting over. "Is it someone I know?"

"In a manner of speaking." He took a bite of bread and mumbled something.

"Sorry?" Penelope kept her face straight. "I could have sworn you just said Brutus."

"Well, the mayor had a business trip to East Asia planned, and since he's not a suspect we can't force him to cancel the trip, and the boarding kennel doesn't have space, and he agreed to sign off on my budget, including the allocation for the youth diversion program, as long as I promised to take care of the dog while he was gone." Jake finished his explanation in a rush and waited.

"And you're telling me because…?"

Jake's shoulder's dropped. "I was hoping you'd be willing to help. I may not be able to get back home to walk him during the day." He stopped when Penelope burst out laughing. "What? He seems like a nice dog."

She nodded. "Oh, he is, but I don't think you know what you're getting into."

"You're not upset?" His face brightened.

Penelope smiled "I'm not the one who's going to be sweeping land mines off the lawn for the next two weeks."

His smile slipped.

Penelope leaned forward and patted him on the shoulder. "I'm sure you'll get used to it."

* * *

AFTER THEY HAD FINISHED EATING, Penelope followed Jake back to his car. "I do need to talk to you about something serious if you still have a couple of minutes." She'd been trying to figure out how much to tell him about what Anne had said. Brian and Anne were friends and she didn't want to put Jake in the middle of their marital difficulties, but Penelope couldn't see any way around it. "I found something out today. It's a little delicate."

Jake's expression became more guarded. "What is it?"

Penelope told him about Anne and the mayor and the men who had broken in. "I don't know if there's some way to have it show up as an anonymous tip or something. The last thing I want to do is hurt Brian, but I don't…" She stopped as Jake held up a hand.

"I'll think of something."

"I'm sorry."

"Me too."

Penelope sighed as she watched him drive away.

PENELOPE SPENT most of the afternoon delivering mail downtown. When she'd applied for the part-time fill-in position, she'd been delighted that competition was fierce for the routes in the newer houses on the edge of town. Those tracts had been built in such a way that the mail carrier could drive up to a structure at the entrance to each cul-de-sac and deliver all the items, including packages, into locked boxes at one spot.

Nobody else wanted the routes downtown, where it wasn't uncommon for a second house to have been built on the back of a large lot, with "1/2" appended to the address number, and a mail slot in the door of the new cottage. Delivering mail to the houses downtown in a timely manner required stubbornness, intuition, and the ability to gracefully exit conversations, all while navigating uneven surfaces, unknown dogs, and gates that were tricky to unlatch.

Penelope loved it.

Not only was she getting paid to walk around the town, but delivering the mail gave her a chance to be nosy in a socially acceptable way. Most of what she delivered was just advertising circulars, but a surprising number of people still subscribed to paper magazines. The divorced dad — she'd delivered the final divorce papers herself — living in the mother-in-law cottage at the corner of Oak and Third with the battered minivan parked on the street, received three different magazines on how to sell fiction, plus a mixture of children's toy catalogs and car magazines. Her ex-husband's divorce lawyer received regular packages leaking glitter, which Penelope assumed were being sent by a spouse of a former client. She did her best to make sure those ones were likely to snag on the mailbox when he took them out.

Penelope got to find out how people wanted to decorate their homes, where they wanted to take a vacation, and how many bills they weren't paying while they dreamed about both of those things.

The best were the postcards. Penelope, like most people, considered it part of the societal contract that anyone was allowed to read postcards. The vast majority were still sent by people on vacation, with some variation on "Everything is wonderful, wish you were here", but on occasion she saw others. There was a brother-sister pair living on opposite ends of the town who had carried on a mild feud for six months by way of postcards, all of which had pictures of cows and a few sentences about a lawn ornament that they kept stealing from each other.

Today, there wasn't much out of the ordinary: a few packages, a few fishing magazines, a lingerie catalog addressed to a house that also received three religious booklets, and a lot of local advertising. A few houses received business envelopes with the same red "Personal and Confidential" stamp on them, which was only odd because the return address wasn't listed. Then she saw something more interesting — a postcard with a photo of a bouquet of chili peppers tied with a strip of lace.

THERE ONCE WAS a copper named Jock,
*   Who ran out with only one sock,*
*   When asked 'bout the tilt,*
*   He just lifted his kilt,*
*   And —*

THE FINAL PART of the closing line had been covered by two different mail sorting stickers, but Penelope was fairly certain she could figure it out without peeling them back. From the amount of wear and tear on the postcard, it had been misdirected at least once, and had probably taken a few weeks to make it to its destination. Penelope had delivered similar postcards to this address before. As usual, the text on the back didn't have a salutation or sender's name, just the limerick, in a neat cursive script that Penelope assumed belonged to a woman, though she recognized that for the sexist thought that it was. The text wasn't always a poem, but it always verged on the edge of risqué.

She gathered the rest of the mail for the address, folded everything around the postcard, and put it in the box, then headed across the grass to the next house. As she walked, a car pulled into the driveway, and she automatically waved. A man got out of the car, and it took her a moment to place him. "Oh, Officer Dolan. How are you?" She waved again and

27

lengthened her stride, trying to look like she was in a hurry so she wouldn't be there when he retrieved his mail from the box.

Only after she was around the corner did Penelope let her laughter out. That was the downside to a job which let her be nosy in a socially acceptable way. Sometimes she found out far more about people than she ever wanted to know.

Penelope pulled the next batch of mail from her bag and promised herself she'd never read a postcard again.

CHAPTER 7

*T*he next morning Penelope entered the police station, detouring around a man reading the riot act to his teenage son. The desk clerk looked at the grey plastic bag, knotted at the top, that Penelope held between two fingers. "Is that what I think it is?"

Penelope smiled. "Probably. Is he free?"

The clerk rolled his eyes and picked up the phone on his desk. "What did he do to deserve that?" he asked as he dialed. "Sir, Ms. Standing is… Thank you." He hung up the phone and hit the button to unlock the door.

Penelope waved and went through, looking to see if Brian was at his desk. Jake had told the detective the story of the assault at the mayor's house, but left the woman's identity a secret, saying that Penelope's source had refused to get further involved. Penelope definitely didn't want to be the one to tell Brian that Anne was being unfaithful, but she was afraid he'd be able to read it on her face the minute he saw her. Luckily Brian wasn't in the room and she was able to make it to Jake's office without interference.

Jake was waiting by his door. "To what do I owe this honor?" he asked after he gestured her into his office.

"You know those clay sculptures you have that your aunt made?" The small figurines looked like a kindergarten project until you looked closer and realized they were poorly rendered imitation netsukes.

Jake took a long breath. "Sadly yes. I promise I'll get rid of them as soon as I can come up with a good excuse."

"Good news. You don't have them any more. Brutus ate them."

Jake blinked. "Is he okay?"

Penelope waved his concern away. "He's fine. The parts I can't account for are small enough to make it through to the other end. Which brings me to the real reason I came by." She aimed for the only clear spot on his desk and dropped the bag with a wet plop.

Jake eyed the sack but made no move to pick it up. "Thanks?"

"I took Brutus for a walk and while I was cleaning up after him I noticed that there was a wad of paper and some fabric in there. It looks like Jezza's picture and some writing on the paper so I thought I ought to bring it in." The picture had been of a younger Jezza wearing a Hooters t-shirt, of all things, and she was standing next to an older man who was posing with a gun. If Penelope hadn't seen the picture with her own eyes, she never would have believed that proper, luxury-loving Jezza had ever held a job much less worked at Hooters. "You probably want to wear gloves. And maybe open it outside."

Jake picked up the bag gingerly. "Thank you."

"I mean, I know it's not the most romantic gift, but you're a really hard person to buy things for…" She ducked her head out the door. "Coast is clear. I'm going to leave before Brian gets back. Dinner at seven?"

Jake nodded, his nose twitching as the smell of the incompletely sealed bag began to permeate the room. "Yes. Oh, and if there's more where this came from…" He held up the bag.

"I will treasure it until we meet again."

Penelope carefully closed his office door behind her, and grinned as she left the building.

CHAPTER 8

From the bay window in Esther's house, Penelope could see the crime tape strung around Jezza's cottage directly across the street, though the wavy glass distorted the image. She wondered who would be responsible for clearing the house out after the police were done with it. She raked through the cat litter and thought about it. Presumably there were people who did that sort of thing. Maybe she could add that to her list. Packing up other people's treasures would be interesting.

"The things you learn about people after they're dead..." Esther's voice trailed off.

Penelope knew that was her cue to stop scooping the litter box and ask a question. "Are we talking about Jezza?"

The old woman repositioned one of her cats on her lap and edged her wheelchair closer. "I had coffee at least one time every week with that woman on the rose garden committee, and not once did she mention having children. I can't imagine what her son thought of me when he came by this morning."

Penelope put the litter box cover back on and snapped

the clasps. "She had a son? Are you sure?" Jezza had never struck her as the maternal type. Of course, she'd never seemed like a Hooters waitress type either. Penelope wondered whether any of what she thought she knew of the dead woman was correct.

"Looked exactly like a younger version of Jezza in drag. Or whatever the opposite of drag would be. He came by this morning to see if Jezza had left any of Brutus's things over here. The poor dog doesn't have anything familiar with him and the police won't let him get anything from the house."

Penelope frowned. "Esther, Brutus is staying with Jake."

"Is he now? Well, I'm glad I forgot about the spare key Jezza had me keep for her then." Her wheelchair hummed as she followed Penelope to the kitchen. She picked up a key from the counter while Penelope washed her hands. "Speaking of Jake, when are you two going to get married?"

Penelope couldn't help laughing as she dried her hands. If Esther went a month without asking her that question she'd call her doctor. "Are we in a rush? It's not like we're going to have a baby out of wedlock or anything. We're fine just the way we are."

"So he hasn't asked you then."

"Well, no."

"Don't let that one get away."

Penelope opened her mouth but couldn't find anything to say. She changed the subject. "Back to Jezza's son. Did he leave a phone number or some way to contact him?"

"It's tacked up on the refrigerator. Do you think I should call him and tell him about the key?"

Penelope poured kibble into the cat bowls and counted to make sure all six cats showed up and ate. "I think you should call the detective in charge of the case and tell him about Jezza's son and give him the key." She wrote down Brian's number on a slip of paper and handed it to Esther. "Do you need me to do anything else while I'm here?"

"Off you go. Tell that man of yours I said hello. And send him over here so I can light a match under his behind." Esther cackled and spun her wheelchair in a circle on her way to the phone mounted on the wall.

CHAPTER 9

*P*enelope followed the pizza delivery driver up the path to Jake's front door. Her feet hurt and all she wanted to do was soak in the bathtub, but she needed to pack her travel bag and head off to a client's house for three nights.

When the driver shifted the insulated box to his other hand he saw her. "Oh hi, Ms. Standing. How are you this evening?" He paused with his finger on the doorbell as Brutus started barking on the other side of the door. "Did you and the chief get a dog?" He took a step back. "Wait, I know that bark. That's Ms. Taylor's big mastiff, isn't it? We stopped delivering to her because of that dog."

Penelope reached into her bag. "Why don't I pay you now and we'll keep the door closed. How much is it?"

He handed her the receipt. "I just need a signature."

Penelope signed the slip of paper, adding a hefty tip. The last thing they needed was a pizza delivery boycott. "We'll make sure he's restrained while he's here, I promise."

"Have a nice night." He handed her the pizza box and ran toward his car.

Penelope counted to ten before opening the door. "Brutus, down." She waited until the dog settled on the floor before going into the house. "Jake, I'm home," she called out. She went into the kitchen and put the whole box inside the oven to keep it away from the dog.

Jake came in from the back yard and washed his hands. "No pottery yet, but there's some crime scene tape and a business card from one of the detectives, so assuming things come out in the same order they went in, I think we should be good."

Penelope set her bag down on top of the refrigerator where it would hopefully be out of Brutus's reach. "Pizza's sitting in the oven. Weren't we going to have that leftover casserole tonight?" The rice, green beans, and ham casserole hadn't been a success, but they'd agreed to stick to the budget in order to save for a camping trip the next month. Or rather, Jake had agreed to stick to Penelope's budget so she didn't feel like she wasn't contributing equally to the household expenses. Working out who paid what, with such disparate incomes, required a balancing act.

"We were, but I took it out to heat it up and then…" Jake tipped his head at Brutus. "My fault, I should have been watching him better. I'll pay for the pizza."

Penelope looked at him skeptically. "Did he eat it off the counter or did you accidentally leave it on the floor and walk out of the room while you ordered the pizza?"

"Would I do that?" Jake looked down at the dog. "She's questioning our motives, big guy. What do you think of that?" He reached down to scratch the dog's head.

The doorbell rang before Penelope could respond. She grabbed Brutus's collar as he scrambled on the linoleum. "Here, hang onto him while I go see who's at the door."

Finding Brian at the door wasn't out of the ordinary, but he usually had a six pack of beer or some chips with him.

This time he stood stiffly on the porch, still wearing his suit. "Hi Pen. I need to talk to Jake about work. Is he here?" He didn't meet her eyes.

"Come on in." She led him into the kitchen. "I'll just take Brutus upstairs with me to pack, and you guys can talk."

Halfway up the stairs, she'd overheard enough to know that Brian had found out whose identity she'd been hiding, and he was offering to take himself off the case. She closed the bedroom door to give them some privacy.

Jake slipped into the room a few minutes later. "Brian's going to stay in the spare bedroom for a few days."

Penelope crammed another pair of socks into her gym bag. "Maybe I should have just not said anything."

"It wasn't anything you did. Jezza and her husband hadn't separated their cell phone accounts yet. Brian was looking through all the calls on the account and saw Anne's number on one of the lines. He put it together on his own." He enfolded her in a hug. "You're off the hook. He's a little pissed at me because I didn't say anything."

Penelope zipped her bag closed and hefted it. "Get him drunk and let him cry on your shoulder." She paused at the door. "You probably want to lock up the guns first, though, so neither one of you shoots the dog when he eats all the pizza." She jogged down the stairs, gave Brian a quick hug as he sat staring at his folded hands, and headed out the door.

CHAPTER 10

*J*ake and Brutus were waiting on the sidewalk in front of the church in the morning. Penelope took in Jake's freshly-shaved face and neatly combed hair. "You're looking better than I thought you would after a hard night of drinking," she said after she kissed him.

"Brutus wagged his tail and knocked over the drinks on the coffee table at about ten, and we decided to call it a night." He tucked a strand of hair behind her ear that had come loose from her ponytail. "How'd you sleep?"

"I have a pink canopy bed with ruffles in the room where I'm staying, the Chihuahua cried to go outside every two hours, and at three in the morning there were cats fighting outside under the window." She rubbed her eyes. "And maybe I missed you just a little."

Jake nodded. "Luckily I had Brutus to fill your job of snoring and accidentally kicking me in the back in the middle of the night."

"I don't snore! And you'll be lucky if the kicking is acci-dental after today."

"Good morning!" Reverend Miller had walked down the steps from the rectory while they were talking. "The two of you look very chipper this morning."

Jake shook hands with the reverend and they exchanged pleasantries. "Brutus and I were just out for a walk, but I was wondering if I could come by later to talk to you."

CJ beamed. "Finally making an honest woman of Penelope then? Congratulations! I'd be honored to officiate."

Penelope snorted. "I'm already the most honest woman he knows."

"Of course you are, and that's why I love you." Jake turned back. "But no, that's not what I wanted to talk to you about. It's a work thing. About your neighbor Jezza."

CJ colored. "Oh dear. I'm sorry. I didn't mean to…"

Jake waved away his apology. "If I can ever get her to say yes, you'll be the first person we talk to."

Penelope leaned back to look up at his face. "I can't very well give you an answer if you don't ask a question."

Jake held up a finger to CJ. "Excuse me for a moment, Father." He turned his whole body to face Penelope. "August 14th. Two-thirty in the afternoon."

She brought out her phone to check her schedule and thought back to where she'd been on that day. "The Cubs game? Wait, you were serious? You were kidding. Weren't you?"

"Is this the face of a man who kids about the Cubs or getting married?"

"I might have to take a Mulligan then."

Jake shook his head. "No points for mixing sports. And I've already done my part. It's your turn." He put a finger on her lips as she opened her mouth. "And none of this 'oh, by the way' business because clearly a big production is needed." He turned back to CJ. "But really I came by to ask if Jezza kept anything in your disaster room."

After one of the Victorian houses had burned down with all the copies of the family's pictures, CJ had opened up one room of the brick and stone church to anyone who wanted to store pictures or documents there for safekeeping. The priest furrowed his brow. "I think she might have left a lockbox there a while back. I can check..." He turned, then stopped. "That is, I can check after the service." He gestured toward the church.

"Of course. I'll give you a call later and set up a time to come by." Jake took off his scarf and snugged it around Penelope's neck. "I'll see you later." He tugged on Brutus's leash and they started walking away. "Big production," he repeated over his shoulder.

Penelope shook her head and went inside the rectory to take care of the needy Dalmatian while CJ went to lead the service.

CHAPTER 11

*P*enelope stumbled to a walk at the end of three miles, the German Shepherd on the other end of the leash glancing up at her and then reluctantly settling down to the slower pace. "Sorry Heidi, we'll go faster tomorrow," Penelope said, massaging the stitch in her side.

"Rough day?" a gruff voice questioned from the other side of the picket fence on the right, startling both woman and dog.

Penelope looked over, then down, finally seeing the elderly man on his knees digging around the base of the lavender. "Some days are a little harder than others," she admitted. She stopped and looked at his face under the wide-brimmed hat. "Mr. Kinsey?" She hadn't seen him in almost two years, ever since he resigned from the city council. "How are you doing?"

"The damned grub beetles are going to kill everything, but other than that I can't complain." He struggled to his feet. "Can I interest you in some lemons? You can take some home to that young man you're seeing."

Penelope smiled at the vision of letting Jake know he was

her "young man". "Thank you, I'll take a few if you have extra." She headed back along the fence to the gate and walked Heidi through, shortening up on the leash to keep her off the pristine lawn. "I didn't realize you lived here," she said as she followed the old man to the back yard where a small orchard of fruit trees provided shade.

"We moved here a few months ago. Had a place in the country but it was getting too much for us." He ducked under a low branch from a fig tree. "Heard you were the one that found that Jezebel woman dead."

Penelope waited a moment, then decided his last sentence had been a question. "Yes. Did you know her?" He was the first person to use her full name, or at least her alias.

"Knew her enough to know I didn't want to know her. Knew her a whole lot less than others." He made a strange choking noise and it was only when Penelope caught up to him on the far side of a heavily laden Meyer lemon tree that she realized he was laughing.

"I think I missed the joke."

He shook his head. "Didn't you ever wonder why everyone on the council agrees to everything he proposes?"

Penelope folded her arms across her chest. "I assumed it was because he was paying them off, but I could never prove anything."

He paused in snipping lemons off the tree. "That's right. You lost your house through that eminent domain scam he cooked up a few years ago."

"What did Jezza have to do with all that?" Penelope folded the bottom of her t-shirt into a pouch and took the lemon he handed her. Whenever the topic of Mayor Harrison had come up in their conversations, Jezza had always made it clear that she'd had nothing to do with his business deals.

"Right after she came to town with her new husband, they made a point of going out to drinks with each of the councilmen. Dinner, drinks, a few more drinks, then a ride back to their place, and then later 'we have some pictures that your wife might find interesting if you don't vote yes on this motion.'"

Penelope stared at him, automatically adding another lemon to the growing pile. "Blackmail?" She'd spent months looking for financial motives, but blackmail had never crossed her mind.

"Oh, they were careful enough to use it rarely, but there it was. I didn't find out about it until last year or I might have tried to stop him. Not that it would have done any good even if I had tried. I don't have any proof, and everyone involved would just deny it." He looked over at her. "Before you decide I'm some paragon of virtue, you should know that his wife's charms were lost on me, and Alex Harrison wasn't committed enough to try for me himself."

Penelope thought about the current makeup of the city council and how the mayor's power had waned since the last election. "Having two unmarried women voted in must have really been a blow."

The gasping laughter returned. "I wish I'd seen his face on election night. Now, can I interest you in a few oranges while you're here?"

By the time Penelope walked Heidi home, her shirt was stretched out by so much produce it resembled a lumpy pregnancy, and she had to stop more than once to pick up escaping fruit. It wasn't until she opened the door and unclipped the dog's leash that she wondered what had happened to all the blackmail pictures.

CHAPTER 12

The town library dated back to 1892. Because of that, the heating was inconsistent, the air conditioning ineffective, and the aisles were kept clear only by ruthless winnowing of the collection twice every year. From the outside, though, it was a beautiful monument to the aspirations of the original founding families. A wide lawn, perfect for impromptu picnics, surrounded the building on two sides, and the third side had the famed rose garden. Membership in the rose garden committee was nearly a requirement for anyone involved in society events, though they were smart enough to leave the plant care to the experts. The fourth side of the building held the wholly inadequate parking lot.

Between the building and the lawns, sturdy benches were anchored to the ground so patrons could read or people-watch. Penelope had commandeered one of them, enjoying the sunshine in peace as she waited for Jake to arrive, while Brutus sniffed everything in a six foot radius.

"Daisy Smith." Jake sat down on the bench next to Penelope, reaching over to scratch Brutus behind the ears. A breeze carried the scent of heirloom roses from the library garden.

Penelope frowned. "I'm gone one night and you've already forgotten my name? This doesn't bode well for thirty years from now. How will I know when your dementia has set in?"

He raised an eyebrow. "We finally got a hit on Jezza's prints. From Interpol of all places. Daisy Smith was accused of extortion in the south of France seventeen years ago, but fled the country before she went to trial." Jake showed her an old mug shot on his phone, the woman clearly Jezza, though much younger. "Did she ever mention anything about France or old friends to you?" He put his phone back in his pocket and leaned back. "And why would it matter when my dementia sets in?"

"Because that's when I'm planning on getting power of attorney and stealing all your money. And no. I don't think she ever said anything at all about her past." Penelope handed him Brutus's leash. "I have a present for you," she said as she unzipped her bag.

"Wait, if it's more dog crap, can you give it to Brian yourself?" He held up a hand as if to fend her off when she pulled out a plastic bag. "I just repaired our friendship, and I'm worried that if I'm the one to give him another bag of poop, he might never forgive me."

"I'd never be that predictable. This is lemons and oranges. You need to eat more fruit during the day." She handed him a plastic bag, the citrus making lumps against the sides. "Brian's working the case again?"

"Investigating Jezza's murder didn't seem like a conflict. If it had been the mayor... Brian would have to recuse himself, and I would, too, since I'd hate to arrest you myself. We'd probably have to call in an outside agency."

"I think your suspect pool is about to get wider." She told

him what she'd learned about the couple's dinner, drinks, and blackmail scheme.

Jake sighed. "Did I ever tell you why I haven't applied for the permanent chief position?"

"Because you don't want to deal with the politics," Penelope responded promptly.

"Because I don't want to deal with the politics. So now we have to go interview every past and present member of the city council and ask if there are incriminating pictures of them floating around." He shook his head. "I might kill the mayor myself when he gets back."

"It's probably good that he already approved your budget."

Jake brightened. "There's that."

"Anything interesting in the reverend's disaster room?" Penelope closed her bag and took Brutus's leash back.

"You know I can't talk about the case but I'm sure the next time you run into CJ he'll tell you that there was an empty box with the lock cut off." He stood up and held out a hand to help her up. "Dinner tonight? Brian offered to grill something."

"Do you promise not to let the dog eat it?"

"Of course. This is going to be good food, not the kind that would accidentally fall on the floor." Jake smiled at her and walked away.

CHAPTER 13

Stopping at her temporary home away from home to let the Chihuahua out before heading over to Jake's for dinner, Penelope opened the door and heard muffled barking. "Chewy, how did you manage to close yourself in here?" she asked as she opened the bathroom door. The ability of certain animals to get themselves into trouble never ceased to amaze her. Case in point, Chewy had managed to get up on the vanity and knock over his owner's aspirin bottle. Luckily the cap was still in place. "Fine, next time you get crated, even if I'm only leaving for a bit."

Chewy had raced past her to the kitchen, and only when she followed him down the hall did she notice that the window on the back door was broken, shards of glass littering the kitchen floor. Penelope felt her blood pressure rising. Having one client murdered was bad enough. Letting someone break in while she was house-sitting — during the same week, no less! — was unacceptable.

The kitchen offered a variety of improvised weapons. Armed with a hammer from the junk drawer in one hand and Chewy in the other, Penelope stomped around the house. "If you're still in here you'd better drop whatever you have and hustle on out the door!"

Everything on the ground floor looked untouched. She went up the stairs, Chewy wagging his tail and trying to lick her face the whole way. The air in the master bedroom tasted stale, as if nobody had been inside in a couple of days. Nobody was lurking in the closet. In the spare bedroom where she'd been staying, the contents of her duffel bag had been upended on the canopy bed. She'd left it neatly packed, as she always did when she was housesitting. There hadn't been much in her bag other than a few clothes and toiletries, and as far as she could tell, they were all still there. Other than her wallet and phone, which she always had with her, Penelope didn't really own much worth stealing. Her son's baby book was in Jake's attic, but even that wasn't worth anything to anyone other than her.

Penelope doubted the burglar had been after a glimpse of her decidedly unsexy t-shirts, sports bras, and underwear with broken elastic, which meant she was going to have to call her client and find out what might have been taken. Gritting her teeth, she called Jake first. "Can you bring one of those property damage forms home with you?" She explained about the broken window.

"The responding officers should have it with them," he said. When she didn't say anything his voice sharpened. "You did call the emergency line, didn't you?"

"I'm sure they're busy with real emergencies. Whoever did this was gone before I got back here." Penelope looked at the hammer she'd set down on the arm of the couch and decided it might be better if she didn't mention how she knew there wasn't anybody in the house.

"Go straight out the front door and wait by the curb. I'm on my way."

"Jake, don't make a huge..." Penelope stopped talking as she realized he'd hung up on her.

* * *

ONE HOUR LATER, after two patrol cars had arrived with sirens blaring, scaring the dog and alerting the neighbors, Penelope was fuming. Four uniformed officers had confirmed what she already knew — the house was empty and the only sign of a break-in, other than the glass on the kitchen floor, was her clothing strewn around the guest bedroom. When she'd reached the owners by phone they'd described the location of all the valuables in the house, and everything was still there.

Since there'd been nothing else to document, and Jake, the acting chief of police, was still present and waiting, the officers had decided that they needed to take pictures of the mess. The longer Jake stood and watched without comment, the more nervous his officers got, and subsequently the more pictures they took, until Penelope put one finger against Jake's chest. "I know you think this is funny, but if you don't stop this soon, Brutus is going to be the only one snoring in your bed for a long, long time." She stomped down the stairs, Jake following behind her. A policeman putting the hammer in an evidence bag distracted her. "Wait. Stop. Where are you going with that? It belongs here."

"We might be able to get prints off it. It was probably what the perp used to break the window."

Penelope recognized the voice and looked closer to see Dolan, the same one whose attitudes had irritated her so much after she'd found Jezza's body. And the one who had received that postcard, though she hoped the decision to forget about that interaction was mutual. "If so, he was considerate enough to put it away afterward. I was the one who got that out."

Jake coughed. "So… you didn't call 911 but you were going to, what, do a little home repair before calling me to get the forms?"

Penelope decided anything else she added would just be digging the hole deeper. "Yes." She crossed her arms and waited for him to comment.

Jake took a deep breath. "You're going to be the death of me." He turned. "Dolan, don't worry about the hammer. The glazier should be here to fix the back door in a few minutes. I need you to stick around until he's done. If there are any problems, call me. I'm going to take Ms. Standing to dinner before there's a second homicide this week." He opened the front door. "After you."

Penelope looked at him, tempted to make him wait. But she'd now interfered with Officer Dolan twice at two different crime scenes, and she didn't want to have to make awkward conversation with the young man while he looked around for something else to bag. Her stomach growled, settling the matter. Squaring her shoulders, Penelope checked to make sure Chewy was still in his crate with his water and his stuffed animals, then walked past Jake and down the front steps.

CHAPTER 14

*A*t three o'clock in the morning, with the streets quiet and no moon to light the backyard, Penelope was having second thoughts about her decision to stay alone in the house. Part of the agreement she had with all of her clients was that she wouldn't invite strangers into their homes while they were gone. That rule had to include her boyfriend, even if he was the acting chief of police. Or possibly *especially* because he was the acting chief, given the things that some people left casually strewn around the house. Still, this was the first night she had ever really regretted that rule.

She could hear Chewy's tags jingling somewhere in the bushes, but an entire army of burglars could be hiding in the darkness and she would never know.

"Come on, Chewy," she hissed. "Let's go!"

The Chihuahua bounded past her into the house, and she locked the door and headed upstairs to go back to bed. Now that the house was empty of people, her brain imagined masked intruders around every corner. She had just turned out the light and slid between the sheets when Jake called.

Penelope pulled the phone under the covers with her. Chewy licked her face. "What's wrong?"

"You weren't kidding when you said that dog needed to go out every two hours, were you?"

Penelope sat up and looked out the window. "Where are you?"

Headlights flashed across the street. "I should have brought Brutus to keep me company."

"You left him at home?" Penelope flopped back down on her pillow. "You'll be lucky if there's anything left of your house when you get back."

"He and Brian were snoring and drooling on each other when I left."

A comfortable silence stretched between them.

"You could go home, you know," Penelope finally said. "I'll be fine."

"I know." His yawn came across the line. "What are you wearing?"

Penelope snorted. "You know exactly what I'm wearing because you watched them take a few hundred pictures of all the clothes I have with me." Safe in the darkness, she smiled. "Oh sorry, were you trying to set the mood?" She was quiet for a minute while her mind wandered. "Why are there so many pineapple fixtures in this house? It's weird."

"Pineapples used to be some sort of symbol of good luck. A lot of the older houses have them." There was a creak of fabric on leather as he settled into another position. "You didn't take anything from Jezza's house the other day, did you? I keep trying to come up with a reason why someone would go through your things. The fire safe wasn't bolted down. They could have carried it away and opened it later, but they didn't bother."

Penelope pulled the covers back over her head. "I guess technically I did sort of take the murder weapon from the scene when I put the leash on Brutus, but I didn't keep it. Maybe someone might have thought that I took all the stuff Brutus ate." She yawned, warm and comfortable in the bed.

"Get some sleep. If you have any problems throw something through the window and I'll be there in seconds." Jake cleared his throat. "It would be a good use for that hammer you stashed under the bed."

Penelope opened her eyes. "How did you…?"

"Good night." Jake was still laughing when he hung up.

CHAPTER 15

*T*he next morning, after drinking a cup of coffee with Spot in the rectory kitchen, Penelope was heading toward her next job when one of the churchgoers stopped her. "Ms. Standing?" The young woman stood next to a new BMW, her hair and clothing immaculate, as if she were heading to a black-tie event and not leaving a small town weekday service. "Can I talk to you a moment?"

Penelope tried to figure out where she knew her from. She wasn't a client, and Penelope was fairly certain she wasn't one of the hundreds that she'd met at various events as part of Jake's job, but her face was familiar. It finally clicked. Not a client, but a friend of her son, one of the girls that had orbited and then spun away during his high school years. "Katie Matlock?"

The woman gave a slight nod and smiled. "It's Whitmore these days."

Belatedly, Penelope recalled her son telling her that Katie had married and dropped out of college, even though she'd been on track to graduate *summa cum laude* with a math and physics double major. The groom had been an older man, if she remembered correctly. Obviously she was doing well materially, but Penelope hoped she'd had the chance to finish her degree in the intervening years. "How are you?"

"I'm fine. Do you have a few minutes to talk? Maybe I could give you a ride home?"

Penelope got in the car and gave directions to Jake's house and by the time they had pulled up to the driveway, Penelope had told Katie how her son was doing and had promised to pass along Katie's greetings.

Katie turned off the engine and waited as Penelope got out. "I have to be somewhere in a few minutes, but… Are you still dating that policeman?"

Penelope nodded. With some people she would have had to bite her tongue to stop herself from giving a lecture about how a woman's worth wasn't defined by the man she was tied to, but she'd seen Katie's expression before. It was her "I really need to talk to someone, but I can't" look. Penelope remembered seeing it the day before a whole group of teenagers had been caught passing out pot brownies to the teachers at school. "I can give you his number if you want to call him."

The woman opened her door and got out. "No, no." She hit a button on her keys and the trunk popped open. "Jezza gave me something to hold for her a couple of years ago. I don't know what's in it, but she didn't want her husband to have it. I don't know what else to do with it." Her eyes darted down, as if the memory were shameful, or just needed to be hidden. "Can I just give it to you?"

"To give to Jake?"

Katie gave half a shrug that turned into a nod. "If you think that's best." She went to the back of the car and pulled out a hefty box wrapped in a black plastic bag secured with old packing tape. Once Penelope had taken it she backed away. "I have to go. Tell Seth I said hello." She climbed back in her car.

Penelope waved, and started moving away. Then another thought occurred to her and she darted forward and waited for Katie to roll down her window. "Was Jezza hanging onto a suitcase for you?" Katie looked like a person who might have an emergency bag stashed with someone unconnected to her daily life.

Katie looked at her for a moment, then nodded.

"I'll…" Penelope stopped before she said the police would let Katie in to pick it up. Katie hadn't stored an emergency bag with a near-stranger because she trusted the police. "If you haven't picked it up by the time the house gets packed up, I'll store it over here until you come get it. Would that be alright?"

Katie nodded again and accelerated before her window was finished closing.

Penelope watched her car disappear around the corner, then went into the house, heaving the box onto the counter to keep it away from Brutus.

"The right thing to do would be to just give it to Jake the way it is right now," she explained to the dog as she scratched behind his ears.

Brutus stared at her.

"You're right, we wouldn't want to waste his time. He's a busy guy. What if it's just Christmas ornaments?" Penelope got out scissors and cut the plastic off.

Under the bag the odor of stale cardboard made her sneeze. She snipped the layer of tape holding the lid on and nudged it up. Her breath caught.

Definitely not Christmas ornaments.

Bundles of hundred dollar bills arranged in a neat layer

met her gaze. Penelope used one finger to push the top layer of cash out of the way and saw another layer beneath it.

Penelope let the lid fall down and stepped back. "That looks like a whole lot of motive."

CHAPTER 16

A sunset picnic in the park with the man you loved was something to enjoy, Penelope thought, even if it did involve a ridiculously large dog and some really cold burgers and fries.

"Sorry," Jake apologized again as he looked at the food in the bag. "I thought I was done for the day and then I got another call."

Penelope put her feet up on the bench and leaned back against him to get a better view of the setting sun. "I knew what I was getting into when you called a timeout on our first date so you could stop a pickpocket." She reached in the bag for another soggy French fry.

"We're suddenly on every law enforcement agency's radar. It turns out that the money in the box is from a bank holdup seven years ago." He threw the rest of his burger to Brutus who swallowed it in one gulp.

"Ugh, you're going to teach him bad habits."

"Do you really think there are any bad habits left to teach him?" He draped his arm around her and pulled her closer.

"Good point." Penelope tilted her head back to look at him. "I bet you're really hoping I didn't skim a stack of that cash and spend it today. Imagine the scandal if you had to arrest me for possession of stolen money."

Jake smiled. "I know you."

"Yeah." She thought about it. "I already have everything I need and I'm pretty content." They watched the red sky for a minute. "Of course... if you arrested the mayor for something I'd be even more content."

"You might be doomed to disappointment on that front. Somehow he found out about our extortion investigation and I think he might have decided to take a permanent vacation. He's abandoned his itinerary and I got a tip that his bank accounts have been emptied. My guess is that he's settling in somewhere on a beach in a country that doesn't have an extradition treaty with us."

"What?" Penelope sat up, sunset forgotten. "Can't you go find him? He should go to prison."

Jake tugged her back down. "I don't think he had nearly as much money as he wanted people to believe, and now he won't be able to come home. Maybe that's punishment enough."

"What kind of attitude is that for the chief of police?"

"Acting chief. And I must be mellowing in my old age."

Penelope threaded her fingers through his. "Next thing you know you'll have to get a light bar installed on your walker." She looked down at Brutus who had given up on getting any more food and was sprawled on the grass. "He left his dog behind."

Jake gave the dog a dubious look. "I'm not completely sure I blame him on that point."

Penelope dropped her head and stared at him.

Jake stroked her hand with his thumb, and the grin he'd

been holding in took over his face. "I'm kidding. Clearly the man is a monster."

"Darn right he is."

Brutus sighed and passed gas.

They watched as the last of the sun's rays glimmered on the horizon to the soundtrack of the mastiff's snores.

CHAPTER 17

Some mornings were just meant to be spent sitting around with a friend. A knock on the back door of the rectory roused Penelope from her spot on the floor next to CJ's Dalmatian. The dog lifted his grey muzzle to glance at the door, then flopped back down. Penelope went over and opened the door to find Jake waiting. She backed up a little to let him by. "Hey, handsome stranger."

That earned her a smile. "CJ's not back yet?" Jake wiped his feet on the doormat on the way in.

Penelope got a coffee cup and poured from the half-full pot. After being there almost every day for years, she was as familiar with the rectory kitchen as she was with Jake's. "He had a meeting with the bake sale committee. Or maybe it was the used clothing roundup committee. Something, anyhow. He should be done in ten minutes or so." She snagged the carton of milk out of the refrigerator on her way to the table and added it to the mug before handing it to him. "Have a seat."

"I still can't believe he pays you to come over every day."

Penelope put the milk away and sat at the table, tangling

her legs with his under the table. "I cut him a deal. He keeps me in coffee and the occasional pastry and I keep his dog company. It's not as if it's a real hardship." She took a sip of his coffee. "Besides, don't you remember what happened the last time I wasn't here?"

A slow smile spread across Jake's face. "As a matter of fact, I do. Quite well."

Penelope laughed. "Not that. I mean here." Spot had howled the entire time and distracted everyone at the service. One of the parishioners happened to be a filing clerk at the station, and she put two and two together when Jake had walked into his office whistling. It had taken weeks for the jokes to stop.

Jake tried to look innocent. "That's what I was talking about. What did you think I meant?"

Heavy steps outside the door kept Penelope from responding.

"Jake, how are you?" CJ went straight to the coffee. "Bless you, my child, for leaving me a cup. I thought we'd never get everyone to agree on how to cater the next movie night." He sank down into a chair at the table. "And then of course we finally decided on a potluck because we always make it potluck." He took a long drink from his mug. "Now is this a personal or professional visit?"

"Professional, my profession." Jake put a hand over Penelope's to keep her from getting up. "Nothing private, just a quick followup. Brian said that Spot woke you up at five thirty as usual on the day Jezza was killed."

"On the dot, same as every morning." CJ explained how his dog could see when Brutus was let out. "Is it important?"

"Well, we arrested two men for drunk and disorderly out at the motel last night." He explained that when the police had looked at their records, one of them had once been arrested with Jezza back when she was still Daisy. "I'm fairly certain we have the ones Anne described — the ones who broke into Mayor Harrison's house last week. We think they were involved in the bank robbery, and they were presumably looking for the cash."

Penelope prodded him. "But?" She knew Jake and he wasn't acting like a man who had arrested someone for the town's only homicide of the year.

"But we have them on a security tape at a convenience store a little before six, twenty miles away. If Jezza was still alive at five thirty, they couldn't have done it and cleaned up in time."

The priest put his mug down. "Brutus barked at people coming up to the house, but I think once someone was inside he would have gone into the backyard for them without a problem." CJ winced. "He's not really a very good guard dog."

Penelope held in a laugh, and Jake patted her hand in acknowledgement of the effort, even as he nodded. "But they would have to have known Jezza's early morning routine." Jake shook his head. "We'll keep looking at them, but I think the killer is still out there."

CHAPTER 18

*P*enelope looked up from the untidy stack of paper in front of her on the kitchen table when Jake came through the front door. "There's spaghetti casserole in the oven if you're still hungry."

Jake dropped a kiss on her cheek as he passed her on the way to the oven. "I forgot I had 'Coffee with a Cop' this evening. Next time I swear we're going to have it someplace I can get something to eat."

"How'd it go?"

"Not too bad." His voice was muffled as he leaned into the refrigerator and pulled out a bottle of beer. "Everyone wanted to know when we were going to arrest someone in Jezza's murder. It was a nice change from the same two people complaining about speeding and the high school kids littering." He pulled the casserole dish out of the oven and sat down across from her.

Penelope scribbled a date on one invoice and moved it to another pile. "This is me not asking how it's going."

"Such admirable self-restraint. Because even if we had

made progress I wouldn't be able to tell you." From the tone of his voice, the case hadn't progressed.

"Where's Brian?"

"Anne came by to see him this afternoon. She wants to get back together." He put his fork down and took a large swallow of beer. "They went out to dinner to talk."

Penelope put her pen down and looked at him. "Did she make that decision before or after she found out the mayor isn't coming back?" The depth of her own irritation surprised her.

"I didn't ask." Jake leaned across the table to touch her hand. "He's a bright guy. It won't be lost on him. We need to stay out of it."

Penelope took a deep breath and blew a strand of hair out of her face. Even if the couple got back together, she and Anne were never going to be going out to lunch again. She flipped another piece of paper into the "done" pile. "Do you think it's safe to cash Jezza's check? They won't have closed her accounts, will they?"

Jake pushed Brutus's nose away from his plate. "Send it in. It's a debt on the estate. If there isn't money in the checking account you'll need to contact her executors." He shook his head. "You know you could put all that on the computer and not have to kill so many trees."

"You sound like my son." She flipped another page. "Ha, you're a good one to talk. This is yours." She slid him a printout with the police department header across the top. "Don't be throwing stones in your glass house, buddy."

Jake frowned at it briefly and pushed it to the corner of the table. "Not guilty. Must be Brian's." He took another bite and pulled the paper back to look at it.

Penelope neatened her stack of checks and put her pen down. "So... I was thinking about something today, but I wanted to run it by you first." She waited.

Jake looked up from what he was reading. "This sounds serious."

"His Honor is not coming back. At some point he'll need to be replaced." Penelope picked up the pen again and toyed with it.

Jake's eyebrows went up. "You're thinking of running?"

"Well, with all the time I've spent trying to fight that bastard, I've learned a lot about how the city works. And I think I'd actually be pretty good at it, if I can get elected." She looked up from the pen and met his eyes. "What do you think?"

"I think you'd be good at it." Jake looked down at the paper again.

"Yes, but what do you think about the idea?"

He looked up and cocked his head. "You aren't really asking me for my permission, are you?" His eyebrows went up. "Who are you and what have you done with Penelope?"

Penelope flushed. "I'm not asking permission. I'm just... it's never come up with us before and... I just don't want to mess up what we have."

"Ah." Jake got up and took his dishes to the sink, then came back around to stand next to her. "I would be honored to be known as the mayor's boytoy."

"Well, you'll have some time to get a name plaque made with that title on it. I still need to get elected." She reached back and hugged him without getting up. "Now are you going to tell me what was on that paper that is so important?"

"It's the schedule for next week's special enforcement efforts."

"Special enforcement? Like DUI checks?"

"That, parole sweeps, speeding hot spots, that sort of thing. Some of the events are publicized in advance, but obviously some aren't. This doesn't have specifics because it's just the info about staffing, but in the wrong hands… And it was printed out the day before the murder."

Penelope stared up at him. "So how did it end up here?"

Jake put his hands on her shoulders. "Are you absolutely sure you didn't take anything from Jezza's that morning?"

"Of course I'm sure!" Penelope shrugged his hands off her. "You think I went through her papers after finding her body?" A thought struck her and she closed her mouth. "Oh…"

"Yes?"

Penelope winced. "The invoice and check. They were paper-clipped together on the counter like they always were and I think I shoved them in my bag before I started cleaning up the mess Brutus made." She rubbed her face. "I'm sorry. I didn't even think about it before now. I must have grabbed the other paper without noticing it."

Jake nodded. "I thought it might be something like that."

Penelope stared at the paper on the other side of the table. "But how did Jezza end up with it?"

Jake's voice was grave. "I'd like to know the answer to that as well."

CHAPTER 19

*A*s anyone with half a brain had expected, Jezza's memorial service was packed despite the early morning hour, all the seats filled even with the partition between the two "slumber rooms" taken down. Curiosity ruled the day, the gossipers watched over by the Morley brothers and their assistant, who had to refill the cookie trays twice before the service started. Conspicuously missing was anyone truly mourning, at least outwardly, although a few people in the front rows had the straight faces of habitual funeral-goers.

As the finder of the body Penelope generated a few whispers. "I guess I should have expected this," she whispered to Esther as she followed in the wake of the older woman's wheelchair.

"Human nature is the only thing that has remained unchanged since I was a girl. Murder creates a spectacle. " Esther gestured to an open spot near the exit and accelerated. "Over there. We can duck out if it all gets too pompous. I wonder if any of these people knew Jezza."

"Maybe not all of them." Penelope wondered if she should

include herself in that group. Prim mayor's wife, brazen bank robber, Hooters waitress, mother, femme fatale, Daisy or Jezza — had she known anything at all of the woman before she died? Mostly Penelope had known that Jezza had a large dog that needed exercise and her checks didn't bounce. It hardly seemed like a fitting testimonial.

Casper Morley, the older and paler of the two brothers, dimmed the lights and walked to the podium. "Per the instructions of the deceased, there will be no eulogy. Instead, we have a presentation that she left to be played during her memorial service." He nodded and the spotlight on the podium faded and a slideshow began playing on two large screens, with the sounds of a pan flute filling the room.

Jezza and her husband at their wedding, both bride and groom smiling; Brutus as a puppy, Jezza holding him in the air; Jezza with her husband at a ribbon cutting ceremony, fashionable pantsuit immaculate.

"Hmph," Esther said, nearly shouting to be heard over the music. "When I go, I want people crying or laughing, not bored to tears watching my vacation pictures. Remember that."

Penelope swallowed her disappointment. When the presentation had started, she'd been hoping Jezza would somehow reveal more of herself after death than she had in life, but it looked like they would only be seeing the carefully crafted image Jezza had maintained. "Do you want any of those cookies before they're gone?" She glanced toward the tray that was almost down to crumbs again.

Facing the other direction, Penelope missed the first different image, but a collective intake of breath from the room snapped her attention back to the screen in time to see Mayor Harrison's naked backside fade out.

Esther's laughter rang out in the suddenly hushed room. "Now it's getting interesting."

Penelope watched, mouth open, as the vacation pictures switched to relatively tame boudoir photos, and then... "Is that Councilman Tanner?" The buzz around the room got louder, drowning out the music, as the images continued. A shriek of rage cut through the room, and a woman in the second row jumped to her feet and started hitting the man next to her with her purse.

Penelope got out her phone and dialed, as Casper Morley ran to the front of the room to stop the presentation, all decorum stripped from him in his panic as he punched buttons on the podium, changing the lights but not stopping the projector.

When Jake answered, Penelope raised her voice to be heard over the pandemonium. "You might want to get down to the funeral home. I think I know where all those blackmail photos are."

CHAPTER 20

Three hours later, ordered chaos reigned in the lobby of the police station, with a man and a woman shouting at each other from opposite corners, and a pair of young Mormon missionaries seated in between, filling out theft reports. Three small children sat on the floor in front of the reception desk, playing with the toys that were normally stored in a basket under the bench, ignoring everything around them. Penelope held up a plastic food container and mouthed "Is he in?" to the unflappable clerk. After a quick phone call she was waved through.

Jake met her in the hallway, tension lines wrinkling his forehead. "You didn't have to come all the way down here." He kept his hand on the small of her back and guided her to his office. "I don't really have time for lunch. This day..."

Penelope pushed the door closed behind her. "Five minutes." The noise from the rest of the station receded although she could still hear a phone ringing. She handed him the container, product of a late night confession when he'd finally admitted his secret comfort food. "Peanut butter and banana on white bread with the crusts cut off. And I won't tell anyone." She stood on her toes to kiss the grey hairs at his temple before sitting on the edge of his desk. "You should take something for that headache."

Jake took a deep breath and slowly let it out, then sat down in his squeaky chair and opened the container. The scent of peanuts filled the office. "I had to put one of my best patrol officers on administrative leave until I can either prove that he printed out that page you took from Jezza's house or prove that he didn't." He took a bite and kept talking. "And with that scene this morning… We have to go back and re-interview everyone, because naturally, before we had photos, every single person claimed that the extortion rumors were baseless lies." He closed his eyes. "I hate politicians."

Penelope cleared her throat.

Jake opened one eye. "Present company excepted, of course."

"Of course." Penelope opened the top drawer of his desk and took out the bottle of ibuprofen that lived next to a pile of pens, staples, and rubber bands. Shaking two out into her palm, she held them out and winced as he dry-swallowed them. "Should I make plans for a candlelit dinner with Brutus or do you think you'll make it home?"

"I'll try, but no promises." He closed both eyes again.

Penelope pushed off the desk. "Understood, but if Brutus eats all the candles in the house you only have yourself to blame." She decided the slight twitch of his mouth counted as a response. "I'm off to see a dog about a run. I'll see you whenever you make it home. Don't forget to drink something other than coffee." She opened the door and headed toward the exit.

Jake's raised voice followed her down the hall. "I love you!"

One of the officers in the hallway, a burly veteran with a buzz cut winked at her. "We love you, too, Chief!"

Penelope left the station to the sounds of laughter.

CHAPTER 21

*H*aving run three miles and safely delivered Heidi back to her house, Penelope decided to enjoy her snack of oatmeal cookies on the library lawn. The heritage rose gardens were in full bloom and the low walls separating the property from the street blocked the wind, making it quite comfortable to sit on the grass and stare up at the sky. Despite the pleasant scene only one other person shared the spot, a thin young man in a grey Georgia Bulldogs sweat-shirt. He sat ten feet away and had the look of a little boy lost in a store, trying to tough it out but on the verge of tears. Penelope was fairly certain she'd never met him, but he looked familiar. It wasn't until he moved his head and a ray of light turned his hair a bright copper color that she remem-bered what Esther had said.

"Excuse me, but are you Jezza's — sorry, I mean Daisy's son?"

For a moment she could see him gathering himself to run, but then he nodded. "Yes, ma'am. Did you know her?"

"A bit." Remembering what her son was like at that age

she moved closer and offered him one of the cookies. "Not as well as I thought I did, I'm afraid."

The corners of his mouth turned up at her last comment. "That just proves she hadn't changed any since the last time I heard from her."

"It had been a while?"

"Three years." He wiped the edge of his eye and lifted his head up. "I got here one day too late."

While they slowly ate the cookies, Penelope extracted his story. He and his mother had worked as a team, fleecing wealthy men as they traveled from one resort town to the next. When he'd secretly applied and been accepted into college, they'd had a huge argument that culminated in Daisy leaving.

"I always thought she might get in touch with me at some point, but I never heard from her. I suppose I shouldn't have been surprised. She always taught me to walk away and not look back."

The stylized bulldog on his sweatshirt caught Penelope's eye. "I think she might have looked back a bit," she said slowly. "One time when I came to walk her dog she had a UGA football game paused on the television. I didn't think anything of it at the time, but she never struck me as a big football fan."

"Not at all."

Penelope nodded. "I don't know if she was looking for you in the crowd or just watching the game because she thought you would be, but I'm pretty sure she was thinking of you."

"Maybe."

They watched a scrub jay land and dig in the grass. "How did you find her?"

"I saw her picture on a website for mastiff owners, and the

location was encoded in the picture. She always talked about finding some rich guy and settling down and buying a mastiff puppy. That was her dream." He gave a weak smile. "I guess she was living her dream. That's good, right?" His smile faded. "But I thought I'd have time, so I waited until I had a week off for spring break. And I was a day too late." He moved restlessly. "I don't even know why I'm still here." He shrugged. "At first, I figured she'd have a stash somewhere, and I might as well look for it, but if the papers are right, that's already been found. I should have moved my return ticket, but I thought maybe I'd learn more about her if I stayed."

Penelope winced. "You weren't at the memorial service this morning, were you?" She tried to imagine how horrified her own son would be if he saw those sorts of photos of her.

For the first time, Jezza's son smiled. "I'm not surprised she arranged something like that. That was my mom. She loved to shock people."

Penelope held out her hand and introduced herself.

He took it, his long fingers wrapping around her entire hand. "Steven. Or, at least, that's the name I've been using for the last three years. It's not my original name."

Penelope settled into a more comfortable position and pulled out her phone to send a text. "There's someone I think you should talk to, but while we wait, tell me about your mother. What was she really like?"

"She could be incredibly selfish, but she could also be really fun. We used to sneak onto boats in the marina and spend the afternoon sailing. When I was little, she didn't mind reading the same book to me about a train that didn't want to go fast, over and over, until the binding broke and she would just hold up a page at a time. Every time she had a lot of money, we would go stay in a nice hotel, and she would give the staff really large tips, and she would promise me that we would go live in a house by the ocean with our own boat and it would just be the two of us and a dog." His smile had a painful edge. "I knew it was a lie. We were there so she could find the next guy. But we would spend hours talking about where we wanted to go."

As they waited for Jake to show up they lounged on the grass and watched clouds float by while Steven told her stories about growing up on the run with the interesting, manipulative con artist who also happened to be his mother.

* * *

THE SUN WAS STARTING to set when Penelope went back into the police station. For once, the lobby was empty, and she was waved straight through. She found Jake in his office, and took some time to observe him before she knocked on the door frame. He was paging through a folder, too quickly to be reading everything, and more as if he was trying to put it all together. While he looked a little tired, he didn't have the lines on his forehead that meant he was fighting off a headache.

Penelope knocked and came in far enough to pick up the plastic container she'd brought the peanut butter and banana sandwich in. "I'm headed home. Should I make extra grilled cheese, or are you and Brian going to be late?"

He looked up. "Sorry, I'm stuck here for a few hours." He sighed. "And Brian is driving around collecting evidence." At her raised eyebrows, he explained. "Someone sent out blackmail notes to everyone we've been able to identify. We're hoping at least one of the notes has useable prints."

Penelope frowned. "But you can't blackmail someone if the pictures have already..." She stopped as she worked it out. "Oh. The blackmailer sent the notices before the memorial service. They must not have known about the slideshow Jezza had set up."

"That's the current theory."

Penelope thought about the memorial service. "The blackmailer must have been upset if they were there." She laughed in spite of herself. "But there was so much going on, it could have been anyone in the room." She shook her head. "Don't stay too late." When he grunted in acknowledgement, she left. But she was only two steps away when she stopped, turned around, and came back. "Those notes weren't in envelopes with a red 'Personal and Confidential' stamp on them, were they?"

Jake let the page he was looking at fall as he lifted his head. "You saw one?"

"I delivered a handful of them."

Jake dug through the papers in the folder, then handed her one. "Anyone that isn't on this list?"

Penelope looked at the list, ticking off the ones she'd delivered, and thought about her route. When she got to one name, she frowned. "Did you say everyone got one? Because there's at least one jerk on here who didn't get one." Thankfully, she'd missed *that* photo at the memorial service.

Jake slowly rested his chin on his hand, one finger holding his upper lip in place, though she could see he wanted to smile. "Can you be a *little* more specific? If I have to track down everyone you've had issues with, I might have to stay all night."

Penelope handed the paper back and pointed. "Scooter Labreque. He's a divorce lawyer." Scooter had convinced her husband to request full custody of their son, which he definitely didn't want, as a bargaining tactic. Up to that point, the divorce had been amicable. After that, Penelope had ended up with far less than half of their assets, but she thought her son's well-being was worth it. "Maybe the letter was delayed, but I delivered all these other ones at the same time. I think everyone else lives on a different carrier's route."

Jake looked at the list. "Interesting."

Penelope raised her eyebrows. "And really, who else would have a stamp that said 'Personal and Confidential' lying around, other than a lawyer? Maybe he killed Jezza to get the photos." That seemed a bit of a logical leap, but the universe owed Scooter some bad luck, even if he wasn't a killer. "Okay, I'm going home to find out what else Brutus has destroyed. I moved your aunt's avant-garde ring holder… thing… lower in the bookcase, but so far he hasn't taken the bait."

Jake already had his phone to his ear when she left, but he was smiling.

CHAPTER 22

*P*enelope had her third cup of hot cocoa in front of her as she sat on the couch, Brutus asleep on her feet, when Jake opened the front door. He left the lights off and removed his shoes before he noticed her sitting there.

"You're still up?" He came into the living room. "What's wrong?"

"Nothing's wrong."

Jake pushed the dog out of the way and sat down next to her. "Eleven o'clock at night, fire in the fireplace, and hot chocolate with marshmallows. You're brooding." He eased an arm around her. "I know you."

Penelope leaned into him and rested her head against his neck, breathing in the scent of him that reminded her of everything good in the world. "I was sitting here hoping that Jezza's son didn't have anything to do with her death even though it means that it was probably someone who lives here. And Brian went to have dinner with Anne again this evening and didn't come back and it's none of my business, but…" She made a noise between a groan and a growl.

"With you on that one." Jake picked out a marshmallow

and ate it. "But I have good news for you. Steven was still in Georgia when his mother died. We checked the flights and there's no way he could have done it."

"That's something, anyway." She sighed. "I'm beginning to think Jezza just wasn't a very nice person. She used her son in her cons while he was growing up, abandoned him, took advantage of anyone who stood in her way, stole, cheated, blackmailed… I think the wonder of it is that nobody killed her before now."

"I've certainly had to ask a whole lot of people where they were that morning." He stole another marshmallow. "A surprising number of them were not where they should have been."

Penelope raised her head to look at him, interest in her eyes. "Anything fun?"

"Did you know that there's a swingers group in town that meets once a month?"

A laugh escaped her. "I know there *used* to be one that met at Sondra Gillespie's house, but that was years and years ago. I can't imagine that's still going on." She looked at his impassive face. "It is? What, do they have a Costco bottle of Viagra next to the bowl of keys?"

Jake raised his eyebrows. "You seem to know an awful lot about this."

Still smiling, Penelope shook her head. "Only second-hand. Sondra used to sit in the back row of the PTA meetings and whisper with one of her friends. I learned more than I ever wanted to know." She drained the rest of the cocoa in the mug.

"Are you done brooding, or should I make you another cup?" Jake stood up and held out his hand.

Penelope let him draw her to her feet. "I think the only thing left on my brooding agenda was how many circus animals I could afford to import." She smiled at his confused expression and twisted to bump him lightly with her shoulder. "I want to make sure the production is big enough."

"Oh, I see." He nudged her backward toward the stairs to the bedroom. "I might have some notes on that I could give you if you're interested."

"Really? Well, if it's not too much trouble..." She took his hand and led him up the stairs.

CHAPTER 23

*P*enelope straightened up after cleaning the last litter box, maneuvering around Esther's chair to get to the kitchen sink without interrupting Esther's story. Things at the service had gone from bad to worse after Penelope had left for her next job, with people screaming at each other and the younger Morley brother getting knocked out by an errant punch as he tried to separate combatants. The projector had been smashed during the melee, though Esther wasn't sure if that had been on purpose or just a result of too many people dodging in a confined space. They had ended up calling for police, fire, and ambulances.

"Did anyone ever figure out who the man in her bedroom was?" Penelope asked when Esther finished. "I'm pretty sure I recognized most of the other people." It had taken nearly two full cycles of the presentation before the projector had been shut down. Penelope was still trying to forget some of what she'd seen.

"I thought all of them were in her bedroom." Esther paused. "I guess it would be easier to set up a hidden camera in your own house instead of a motel. Or a la carte." She stopped. "No, I don't mean 'a la carte'. What do I mean? The fancy way to say getting busy outdoors."

"Al fresco?"

"That's it! Al fresco. It would be hard to hide a camera. And the squirrels might take it."

"I can't say I've ever thought about it. You might be right." Penelope grabbed a paper towel to dry her hands. "But I meant the house across the street." Then she realized that Esther might never have been inside, since it hadn't been retrofitted to accommodate a wheelchair. "The picture in the room with the twining ivy wallpaper."

"Ah, the one with the very young man with his face hidden by the pillow. No, I didn't hear anything about who he might be."

Penelope got stuck on what Esther had said. "How do you know he was young?" *She* hadn't noticed much other than a naked man on a bed in a room she recognized.

"Angles, dear. In case you hadn't noticed, things change as men get older." Esther laughed as she wheeled over to the kettle. "That picture *was* different, though. Perhaps he was an actual boyfriend. He certainly couldn't have been old enough to be worth blackmailing."

Penelope made a face as she accepted the mug of chamomile tea and sat down at the tiny formica table. "Can you imagine? You'd have nothing to talk about."

Esther settled in across the table with her own drink. "Perhaps she didn't talk to him much. But I agree. It takes half a century to civilize them to the point of being good company." She blew across her mug and raised her eyebrows as she looked at Penelope.

"Jake's excellent company, yes." Penelope tried for a look of innocence as she stared up at the ceiling.

Esther sighed and shook her head. "Rumor has it he's

waiting for you to propose to him. I suppose it's a sign he's enlightened or something."

A few drops of tea splashed onto the table when Penelope put her mug down. "Since when do you and CJ gossip about people?"

"Since the two of you need a swift kick in the pants to make it official. What are you waiting for? You're crazy about each other and the finances would work out better for both of you."

"He wants a big production. I'm trying to figure out what that means." Penelope sipped her tea. "On a budget," she added, as Esther opened her mouth.

"What's wrong with dinner, candles, wine, and wandering hands?" Esther's laugh was drowned out by the roar of a car racing down the street.

Penelope hid a smile as she glanced over to the window. "These older houses really let the noise in, don't they?"

"That's one thing I won't miss about Jezza. She used to race down the street like a bat out of hell. She must have had a stack of tickets up to her waist."

Penelope finished her tea and got up to wash out her mug. "Do you need anything else before I go?"

"No, but if you don't have a good plan for this big production by tomorrow, I swear I'm going to arrange something myself."

Penelope choked back a laugh. "I'll figure it out, don't worry." She let herself out the side door and walked to her next client, watching the cars as they drove by.

CHAPTER 24

The more she thought about it, the more Penelope liked Esther's idea, at least the dinner and candles part. True, Jake was in the middle of a homicide investigation that had snowballed to include bank robbery and blackmail, but if it wasn't that, there would be something else. If she waited for a more quiet moment, she might wait forever.

First things first — if she was planning a romantic dinner for two she had to make sure both people would be there and nobody else. Penelope scrolled through the contacts on her phone and frowned. She had Anne's number but not Brian's. Given her last conversation with Anne, she didn't want to go through her, even if Anne and Brian where back together. Penelope had no idea which way *that* wind was blowing. The guest bedroom door had been closed when she'd left in the morning.

Penelope dropped in at the police station between two dog walking assignments. Luck was with her. Brian was at his desk typing on the computer.

"I have a big favor to ask," she said when he looked up.

"I'll warn you right now, I don't have the key to the

evidence locker," he said. "But anything other than that is yours."

Penelope sat down at the chair next to his desk. "I need a couple hours alone with Jake this evening," she said in a voice low enough that it wouldn't be overheard. Not that any secret ever stayed hidden long in the station, but she could make the effort.

"No problem. I'll go out for a drink with the guys. You can text me when it's safe to come over."

"And I need you to make sure that Jake makes it out of here on time." She saw his doubtful expression. "I know, but can you at least try to make it happen? I'll leave you some Chicken Kiev and cherry cobbler if you come through."

Brian leaned back in his chair and played with a rubber band. "Bribing a cop has some serious penalties, but if you promise to make lasagna some day soon, I'll overlook it. What time do you want him home by?"

"Seven." She stood up.

"I'll do my best."

"Thanks."

Knowing that Jake would wonder about her visit if she didn't stop in, she went back the hall to his office where she found him on the phone. He covered the lower portion with one hand. "Do you need me?"

She shook her head. "Just passing by. Dinner at seven?"

He glanced at the chaos on his desk. "I'll try. I'll text you if I'm running late."

Penelope blew him a kiss and left.

* * *

ONE ROUND-THE-BLOCK ELDERLY POODLE STROLL, a three mile jog with Heidi, the German Shepherd, and one extended trip to the dog park later, Penelope had a hole in her schedule just long enough to make it to the grocery store and back home. As she passed the church, CJ was standing on the sidewalk next to Esther in her wheelchair, his Dalmatian lying in the grass by his side.

Esther broke off whatever she was saying when she saw Penelope. "Why didn't you tell me they were about to arrest someone? I had to hear about it from Georgina when she called about the rose garden chili cook-off."

With a quick glance to make sure there wasn't any traffic, Penelope jogged across the street and gave Spot a quick ear scratch. "For Jezza's murder?"

Esther looked up at CJ and shook her head. "How can she live with the man and know less than the rest of us?" She looked back at Penelope. "Yes. They arrested that lawyer with the name that sounds like a car."

Penelope had known Esther long enough to puzzle that one out easily enough. "Scooter Labreque?" When Esther nodded, Penelope raised her hands above her head as if she was crossing a finish line. "Yes!" She let her arms drop back down. "He's an awful person," she said to CJ, realizing her levity might be a little out of place.

"He was the one who broke into Jezza's lockbox in the disaster room." CJ sounded aggrieved. "I could understand that action if he had just been trying to make sure his own pictures didn't get out, but then he went and blackmailed all those other people." He stopped suddenly as if remembering his vocation. "I'm sure he'll receive forgiveness from the Lord if he repents." From the reverend's tone, God might forgive Scooter, but the lawyer was going to have to work a lot harder to get CJ on his side.

Penelope looked at Esther, who seemed to have the most information. "Did he confess to the murder?"

"Of course not. He's a lawyer. Lawyers never confess, especially if they're guilty." Esther shook her head. "But

Georgina said he didn't have an alibi. She lives three houses down from him, and she sees him riding his bicycle every morning. He could have easily killed Jezza and then ridden home without anyone the wiser."

Penelope suspected they had to have more evidence than that. She bent down to scratch Spot's ears again. "I'd offer to tell you anything I learn when I see you tomorrow, but I'm guessing you'll know it all long before I do." She straightened. "I'm off to buy groceries. Do either of you need anything?"

The reverend shook his head. Esther smiled. "And candles?"

CJ raised his eyebrows. "Big plans tonight?"

Penelope returned Esther's smile. "And candles." She waved and dashed across the street again, making a mental list of everything she might need.

JEZZA'S SON, Steven, was in line in front of her in the grocery store, buying a sandwich and chips. He glanced at her when she got in line and grinned. "Penelope! I'm glad I ran into you before I left. Did you hear they arrested someone for my mom's…?"

Penelope nodded. "I just heard."

"I'm glad. I know it won't bring her back, but I feel better knowing he won't get away with it."

Penelope nodded. "Are you heading back to school soon?"

"Yes, but I'll be back when they release my mom's things. I guess it might be a while, with…" He waved with the arm not holding his items, "well, everything."

Moved by the impulse to be a better friend to Jezza in death than she had in life, Penelope gave him her phone number. "Let me know when you're coming back and I'll arrange things on this end."

When he had paid and left, the cashier watched him go. "That was her son, wasn't it?" She paused with the package of chicken breasts in one hand. "I still can't believe everything his mother was getting up to. She made a joke a few weeks ago about having a get-out-of-jail-free card, but I thought that meant she was dating a cop. I didn't realize it meant she was blackmailing half the men in town." She started scanning Penelope's purchases. "Big night with the chief, hm? Can't go wrong with candles and wine."

Penelope sighed and nodded and thought that Jake might be the last person in town to find out about their dinner.

CHAPTER 25

*P*enelope looked around at the kitchen and ran through her mental list. Table set with the nice tablecloth, candles, and flowers — check. Wine open — check. Chicken breasts pounded, rolled up with butter, breaded and in the refrigerator awaiting frying — check. Broccoli (to magically counteract the hardening of their arteries from the Chicken Kiev) washed and ready to be steamed — check. Dog fed and bribed to stay in the other room with treats — check. Bread in the oven, waiting to be warmed — check. Only evening dress she owned, black velvet with an apron pulled over it to keep it clean until she was done cooking — check. No Jake yet, but it was still ten to seven and he hadn't called or texted to say he'd be late, so she had started heating the oil.

Her phone rang, an unknown number. "Hello?"

"Pen, it's Brian. Sorry to bug you, but Jake went to the gym to go work out a while ago and his admin needs him to sign something tonight for the payroll so it can get faxed before midnight. If I call him he'll come back here and then we both know he'll never get home on time, so I'm just going to send it over with one of the patrolmen. Don't panic if a uniform knocks on the door before he gets there."

That last sentence explained the call. "No panic, I promise. And thank you." She hung up and caught a glimpse of her reflection in the window. Her hair was all over the place and there was something on the shoulder of her dress where the apron didn't cover it. She dashed to the mirror and found that she'd managed to get butter smeared on one spot while the left elbow had been breaded. So much for the evening dress.

Penelope jogged upstairs, yanking the dress off along the way, slipped into a skirt and pulled on a blouse, buttoning it as she went down the stairs. It wasn't until she was at the bottom of the stairs that she saw the patrolman standing on the other side of the clear glass panes of the front door. His frozen deer-in-the-headlights stare made her wonder how much of that journey he'd been present for.

Penelope decided she'd just have to brazen her way through it. She opened the door. "Officer Dolan, isn't it? Come on in. You have some papers for Jake to sign?"

"Yes, ma'am." He took off his hat and came through the door, hugging the wall the furthest from her. Brutus came out from the spare room, sniffed the policeman's shoes for a second, then trotted back to his treats. "If the chief's not here I can go wait out in the car."

"Nonsense, have a seat. Would you like something to drink?" Penelope didn't really want to entertain someone when she was trying to get everything ready, but she didn't want to be rude. That thought reminded her of their conversation a few days ago. "Look, I'm sorry I didn't tell you who I was when you took all my information after Jezza was killed. I hope it didn't cause too many problems when you called the chief to confirm my whereabouts that morning."

"No, ma'am. Everyone thought it was funny."

She might have believed his even tone, but a muscle twitched at the corner of one eye. And if he didn't stop kneading his hat with those beefy fingers he was going to destroy it. "Well, I apologize anyway." A silence strained the room as he sat gingerly on the couch.

The front door opened, saving her from further awkwardness. Jake came in, scratched the dog's ears when he trotted over, and put down his bag. Penelope leaned into his embrace, enjoying the smell of soap and sunshine. "You forgot to sign some papers before you left the office."

"So I see." He looked her up and down. "Looks like I should have hurried straight home."

Penelope left the two men in the living room and turned the oven on. "At least now we know how to keep Brutus calm," she called from the kitchen. "He was more interested in his treats than he was about a stranger coming into the house. I thought he was going to tear down the door to get to the UPS guy yesterday." The oil bubbled slowly when she dropped a cube of bread in. Another few minutes and it would be at the right temperature.

She wandered back out to the living room where Jake was handing over the freshly signed papers. Penelope moved to the door, hoping to hurry the officer on his way. She thought he'd likely leave quickly anyhow. Clearly she made him nervous, although at least he'd stopped mangling his hat. Those fingers reminded her of something though…

Dolan got up and picked up the sofa cushion that had tipped over and she had it. The picture from Jezza's service, the only one taken in the new house, with a man's face covered by a pillow. The man in the picture had those hands.

Brutus hadn't reacted to a stranger because Dolan wasn't a stranger.

"It was *you* —" Penelope's eyes widened and she accidentally made eye contact with Dolan as he walked toward her.

With just a slight catch in her movements, she plastered a smile on her face. "Thanks for bringing the —"

The breath was knocked out of her as he grabbed her and spun her around, pulling her against his chest. Penelope saw Jake freeze at the same time she felt a cold metal barrel touch her temple.

CHAPTER 26

*P*enelope froze, watching the blood drain from Jake's face across the room.

"Put your hands where I can see them!" the officer growled at her ear.

She lifted her hands to eye level before realizing he was talking to Jake. "Oh, sorry," she said as the man behind her moved his head to see around her arm.

Jake held his hands out to the side. "Take a deep breath and think about what you're doing."

"Why do you always screw up *everything*?"

"Well, you said to put my hands..." She trailed off as Dolan's breathing got harsher. "Oh, you mean the other stuff. That was mostly on accident."

"I spent *hours* making sure that everything about that scene pointed to her husband, and you went and cleaned it up."

"Put the gun down and we'll talk," Jake said, his voice perfectly level.

"In my defense, that was mostly Brutus who messed it up."

Dolan kept talking, the gun unmoving at her head. "I even

made footprints with an old pair of his shoes that she kept for gardening. And then you destroyed it all."

Penelope took a breath to defend herself and closed her mouth when Jake looked at her. Perhaps it wasn't the right time to force Officer Dolan to accept her point of view. "You didn't mean to kill her, though, did you?" At least if he was talking he wasn't shooting her. "I mean, strangling someone with a leash doesn't scream premeditation."

"She laughed at me."

The whirr of the kitchen fan was the only sound for a few seconds.

Penelope reached up to pat the arm restraining her. "I'm sorry. That must have hurt."

"I thought she loved me. I did things that would have ruined my career for her. It started out with just fixing a few tickets, and then she wanted me to find out things about people and cases, but that was okay because we were going to go away and start again somewhere else where nobody knew us." He choked out the last few words.

Penelope tried to read the signs from Jake's face. Was he encouraging her to continue, or was that a look telling her not to make the guy with the gun start crying? While they'd worked out a signal for when they needed to be rescued from a conversation at a party, they'd never worked out a hostage strategy. That seemed like a grave oversight at the moment. "What's your plan now? Too many people know you came over here tonight. Jezza was an accident and a good lawyer will be able to work something out. Why don't you put down the gun and we'll talk about it." The smell of overdone bread wafted out of the kitchen.

His voice took on a dreamy quality. "There's nothing left for me anymore. Everything's ruined."

"Don't talk like that," Penelope said, calling on what her son called her "mom tone". "We'll get you a lawyer and everyone will sit down and talk, and you'll get a good night's sleep, and things will look better in the morning."

She could feel him wavering. His arm loosened and the hand with the gun moved slightly away from her head. "Do you really—"

At the sudden blast of sound from the smoke detector above his head, Dolan started and Penelope felt a pain in her forehead as the gun went off.

CHAPTER 27

*W*ith the shot ringing in the ear already deafened by the smoke alarm, Penelope threw her hands up to protect her head, one arm knocking the gun out of Dolan's hand. She felt, more than heard, the gun clatter on the hardwood floor and dove to the ground to cover it with her body. With it safely digging into her stomach she looked over to where Jake had been standing, but he wasn't there. She scrambled forward, one arm cradling the gun against her body, to check the floor where he'd been.

Only when she saw the empty space did she notice the commotion behind her, and by then Jake already had Dolan on the ground, using the younger man's own handcuffs to restrain him. Penelope sagged to the floor in relief, at which point she realized that blood was dripping onto the floor from her head. Indignation overwhelmed her. "He *shot* me."

Jake was already on the phone calling for backup and an ambulance, yelling to be heard over the alarm and trying to fend off the excited Brutus with one arm. He finished restraining Dolan and crouched down next to her, reaching out to touch her head as if she were delicate porcelain. "You okay?"

"I think so." She lifted the hand pressed against her wound. "How bad is it?"

His relieved smile told her everything she needed to know. "Just a scratch."

They didn't even have time to silence the smoke alarm before the first police car arrived.

* * *

A LITTLE WHILE later Penelope sat on the couch, snuggled into Jake while a paramedic finished putting a butterfly bandage on her head. Through the front window she could see the fire truck backing out into the street, threading a careful path between almost every police car the city owned and a gaggle of pedestrians. Brutus howled his displeasure at being locked in the back yard, Dolan was sobbing in the back of a squad car, and the whole living room was being documented as a crime scene. The room smelled of overheated oil and burned bread, but at least the smoke alarm was no longer blaring.

"This wasn't exactly what I had in mind," she said and winced from the additional pressure as gauze was applied. "But if you were looking for a big production, I'm not sure I could have managed anything bigger. So... Will you marry me?" She snuck a glance back at him and found him staring at her in disbelief.

"Really? You want to do this now?"

"Well, I was going to ask earlier but I didn't want you to try to wiggle out later and claim that it wasn't fair because someone was holding a gun to your head. Even though technically the gun was to my head not yours." She tapped the bandage.

"I worry about you."

"Is that an 'I worry about you, yes' or an 'I worry about you, no'?"

"That's an 'I love you, yes', but I swear if you ever start arguing with someone holding a gun to your head again..." His arms tightened.

With a contented smile Penelope relaxed into his embrace and watched the chaos around her.

EPILOGUE

From the *Newtown Gazette*:
Former Police Officer Sentenced To Seven Years

Former patrolman Alan Dolan pled guilty and was sentenced to seven years for the second degree murder of Jezza Harrison under a plea deal worked out by the prosecutor on Friday.

Under the terms of the plea deal, Dolan read a statement in court expressing his regret for his actions. At the time of the murder he was in a relationship with the deceased, the ex-wife of the former mayor, Alex Harrison. The victim's former husband fled the country to escape prosecution in an unrelated matter.

The son of the victim was in court for the sentencing. He had no comment.

Standing-Wheeler Marriage

Penelope Standing, age not given, married Jacob Wheeler, age not given, in the backyard of the Wheeler residence on

Saturday. The Reverend CJ Miller, a long-time friend of the couple, presided.

The bride wore a vintage purple silk dress with a bouquet of wildflowers picked from the yard by her grown son, who also walked her down the aisle.

The bride promised to love and honor the groom and "try to not argue with armed people". The groom promised to "love and honor Her Honor", a nod to the bride's status as the newly sworn-in mayor. A slight delay occurred after it was discovered that the couple's dog had eaten both rings, but suitable replacements were found and the ceremony finished without further difficulty.

The reception was held in the house immediately after the ceremony. The couple did not disclose their honeymoon plans.

ACKNOWLEDGMENTS

Even though there weren't many people directly involved with this novella, it would be a lie to say that I did this without a lot of support. Whether I needed emergency punctuation advice, or just to know that I wasn't the only one writing at dawn, my writing community was always there for me. You all are awesome.

My brother, Eric, looked over the final version of this manuscript, and thus is completely responsible for any remaining typos. He was also kind enough to point out a few flaws, and strongly suggested that if I referred to a character over thirty times, he probably ought to have a name. His input helped make this a stronger book, even if he doesn't know *anything* about dog toys.

ABOUT THE AUTHOR

Tess Baytree is the pen name of speculative fiction author T. M. Baumgartner. At various times she has been a veterinarian, Unix system administrator, software developer, and after-hours book-shelver in a medical library.

Theresa currently lives in Northern California in a house with too many animals. She knits hats for garden gnomes and runs with scissors only when absolutely necessary.

ALSO BY TESS BAYTREE

As Tess Baytree:

Death Tracks the Scent

As T.M. Baumgartner:

Shift Happens

The Chaos Job (Jackpot Drift #1)

The Chaos Connection (Jackpot Drift #2)